The Dark Legend of the Foreigner II

The Dark Lords

Frank DeStefano

LifeRich Publishing is a registered trademark of
The Reader's Digest Association, Inc.

LifeRich Publishing books may be ordered
through booksellers or by contacting:

LifeRich Publishing
1663 Liberty Drive
Bloomington, IN 47403
www.liferichpublishing.com
844-686-9607

ISBN: 978-1-4897-1232-5 (sc)
ISBN: 978-1-4897-1231-8 (e)

Library of Congress Control Number: 2017904372

Print information available on the last page.

LifeRich Publishing rev. date: 4/12/2022

The Dark Legend of the Foreigner II

Chapter 1

It had been a few months since Matt Rider and his cohort had seen The Master. Ever since his appearance at Saint Patrick's Cathedral in Manhattan on his wedding day, Matt had wondered how he could still be alive and, more importantly, what he wanted. *Is revenge on his mind?* he asked himself. *More than likely it is.*

Matt wasn't thrilled that The Master had jumped on a truck that carried a secret military robot named Nemesis. Only a few select people knew about the Nemesis project, a project that had gone bad. It was merely coincidental that the military happened to come by at the same time The Master had exited the church. Then, conveniently, he had disappeared. How did someone who looked like he did—with gleaming skull and red eyes—just disappear so easily? He had ruined Matt's wedding day. But The Master didn't care about that. He only wanted revenge.

After Matt and Sherry got back from their honeymoon, Matt started looking for the Master, but it was as if he were a ghost who had come and gone in a single breath. He wasn't anywhere to be seen, and no one could find him. It seemed impossible that this could happen.

Matt thought it strange that reports had it that Albert Herr and his father, John Herr, were gone as well. The two were archeologists and had been working on a time machine. Matt had looked into that, and after some research, he discovered that it seemed as if Albert and his father had been linked to The Master for some time.

One Thursday afternoon, Matt and his wife Sherry took a drive to a building at Chelsea Piers in order to learn more. They shut the door to the GMC Yukon and walked up to the building, not knowing what to expect. From the outside, the structure looked as if it had been deserted for months. It was broad daylight, but Matt and Sherry kept their guns just within reach and not far from their waists. An older man approached them and began to question them, but he backed off when he realized who they were.

The boarded-up building looked like something a gang would use, not a pair of archeologists. After asking a few pertinent questions of the older man, Matt and Sherry went inside. There they found robot pieces all over the place, scraps of metal and wiring. The disarray on the floor was evident, as was the destruction. The whole warehouse was a complete mess.

Matt and Sherry looked at each other, a shared look of panic crossing their faces. On a desk, they found notes that had been scribbled on and crossed out. As they walked around, they knew something had gone terribly wrong. Matt had thought their darkest days were behind them, but this looked bleak.

More disturbing were the body parts of machines. It looked as if Albert had done an extensive makeover on a very large robot. Matt picked up a robot hand to inspect it more closely. His biggest fear was that somehow The Master had gained control over both Nemesis and the Herrs.

"Do you think that the Herrs helped The Master?" Sherry asked, pulling at the end of her long red hair.

"I don't think so," Matt said.

"Well," Sherry said, "you just don't know." She knew that Matt had a good heart and always thought the best of people.

Circuit breakers and a multitude of wires lay in the dust-filled laboratory. Searching the warehouse, Matt and Sherry found large boxes that had been covered up, and many computers set up and ready for use. Matt didn't quite know what to make of it all, and neither did Sherry. It seemed as if the Herrs had built something or taken something apart; or perhaps both. They had done a decent job of hiding whatever it was they were doing.

As the new police commissioner, appointed as such shortly after his father's death, Matt had a responsibility to watch over the city. He realized that something was up, but he didn't know what it was, and it scared him. He and Sherry walked up a few stairs to where there was a desk and a computer set up. Matt discovered some papers with different formulas written on them. The writing looked like chicken scratches or a doctor's handwriting. All the papers were like that, and Matt couldn't read them. It was as if the writer were trying to recreate something that perplexed him, and had started over and over again. It was very confusing, and Matt wondered about its meaning.

Sherry took a look but couldn't make sense of the writing either. She took the papers and put them in her pants pocket.

They walked around the floor, Matt on one side and Sherry on the other, then did the same downstairs. Matt picked up a circuit breaker and took it with him as they left the warehouse.

The elderly man who had greeted them earlier saw them leaving. "Did you find what you were looking for?" he asked.

Sherry said they hadn't.

"Too bad," he said. Then he added, almost under his breath, "The Chinese man left with two hooded figures on a boat."

"What? Say that again," Matt responded. "What Chinese man? Maybe you'd better show us the log."

"I just patrol the dock," said the elderly man. "Let's go to the dockmaster."

Matt and Sherry followed him to the dockmaster's small shack. When he opened the door, the dockmaster's body fell out, and Sherry covered her mouth in shock. Matt crouched down to examine the body. He estimated that the man had been dead for about two days.

The elderly man simply raised his hands to his temples, unable to comprehend what he saw.

Sherry and Matt looked at each other. "Now it starts," he said. Matt grabbed the logbook that was on top of a shelf and handed it to Sherry, then eased the body out of the shack. Then he called his precinct.

Looking through the book, Sherry came to an empty page. "Why isn't there anything written here?" she asked.

The elderly man, still in shock, muttered that he wasn't sure.

They heard people calling for help, and Matt spotted two men tied up near the end of the dock. He ran over, took out his knife, and cut the ropes to free their arms and legs. He took the tape off their mouths, and as the men caught their breath, he asked, "Who did this?"

"Two hooded men and some Chinese man."

"What!" Matt exclaimed.

The victims who had been bound confirmed that one of the men was called Albert, and that he had taken one of the boats.

"Where were they headed?" Matt asked.

"No idea," one of the men said. The other chimed in, "All he said was, 'cold fusion, cold fusion.' What the hell is that?"

The two men were eventually free to go, and just then, Jack Rider, Matt's brother, and Takeo arrived. Sherry showed Jack and Takeo the empty space in the logbook, and explained about the hooded men and the Chinese man.

"Where are they headed?" Takeo asked. His English had grown nearly perfect after much practice.

"We don't know," Matt said.

Takeo put his hand on Matt's shoulder. "Don't worry," he said. "We'll find him."

"Yes, but now we know The Master has control over Nemesis, and we have no idea where he's going. This is just wonderful." Matt was pissed off. He had a city to watch out for, after all.

He asked Sherry for the pages with the formulas and eagerly showed them to Jack and Takeo.

"This can't be good," Jack said after glancing at the pages.

Takeo murmured assent; he also sensed that something deadly was on the rise, and that gave Matt a bad feeling, though he had no idea what was coming.

Matt and Sherry got in their SUV and drove off. Jack and Takeo waited until the body was taken away before leaving.

When Matt and Sherry arrived at the precinct, Matt showed the formulas to one of the police officers. He couldn't make out the handwriting either but agreed to have it analyzed. Matt went back to his desk and decided to do some research and input the formulas, as nearly as he could decipher them, into the computer. None of them garnered any results.

Two hours later, the police officer who had been examining the formulas finally called Matt. He and Sherry went downstairs.

The officer handed the formula to Matt and shook his head. "Matt, you really don't want to know."

"Just tell me what it is," Matt said as Takeo and Jack walked in.

"It's a formula for cold fusion."

Matt had no idea what cold fusion was. They all looked at each other, confused. None of them had ever heard of it. "What is that?" he finally asked.

The officer looked it up online. After a few tries, he came up with several pages of links. He clicked on one.

Matt leaned over his shoulder and began to read. One article in particular read:

Cold fusion is a type of nuclear reactor, a tool with many dangerous consequences, which can create an immensely powerful set of conditions that end in catastrophic results.

Matt handed the circuit breaker he had taken from the warehouse to the officer.

"What's this?" the officer asked.

"Found this circuit breaker in the Chelsea Piers building."

"Do you have any idea where The Master could have gone?" the officer asked.

Matt shook his head.

"Even if you did, catching him in open water would be impossible. He's going to get what he's going to get."

"Look, he's right," Jack said. "There's no way of detecting where the formula could have come from?"

The officer said he had checked, but the problem was that there were so many European countries looking into it that trying to find one that would fit the profile would be dangerous.

"Seriously," Matt said, "how can we stop him? It's not only him I'm worried about. It's who he will step on in the process of trying to get what he wants."

"Matt," the officer said, "know that whatever happens, you will have to let the fate of someone else fall into their own hands. Look at the screen and see how many countries have possible links to cold fusion."

There were dozens or more.

Jack said, "It's impossible."

Takeo looked perplexed. It was an intimidating experience for someone who didn't really understand the finer details of science.

"I'm going for a walk," Matt said. As the new commissioner, he had a lot weighing on his mind. He had one of the largest cities to defend and to protect, and The Master now alive and at large was just an added complication. He had no idea how it was even possible, though he knew he needed to figure it out, and quickly.

Takeo went after him as if to stop him.

Sherry reached out to grab his hand. She shook her head and said, "Don't bother." Takeo let Matt walk away.

Sherry knew of Matt's tendency to get aggravated easily if he couldn't figure something out. In this case, it was impossible to determine where The Master was headed. Matt and the crew felt certain that The Master and the Herrs weren't in New York. That would be a major concern after all the devastation the city had seen of late, so Matt was happy that they weren't. However, Matt knew something big was going to come from this. A military robot named Nemesis that had gone bad and had way too many problems with its design didn't bode well. It had been tested in Area 51. It was supposed to stop any terrorist attacks, or anything that might threaten the American people.

But it wasn't easy for the U.S. government to shut this project down. Millions of dollars had been spent trying to make him the perfect android. But no one truly knew that it had been built to protect the lives of humans. It was something that wasn't going to be easy to get back, a war machine that was impossible to destroy. It was funny, in a way, that The Master had gotten someone like Albert on his team, with such power, intelligence, and technical capabilities. With that added alliance and The Master's already dangerous abilities, the future of the world was no doubt in great jeopardy.

Takeo was still new to the world he currently inhabited, and he had a lot to learn. Many things were different from the world he had known. Takeo had been a great warrior, a samurai with all the accompanying gear. Getting dressed each morning in a police uniform struck him as odd. He thought that eventually he'd get used to it, but he hadn't yet.

Despite the drastic changes in his life, he mused that at least he was alive and well.

Chapter 2

Matt didn't know how the Master had gotten away, and neither did the rest of the crew. Takeo had an idea, but he wasn't too sure. Back at the precinct, Matt confronted Takeo. Takeo knew many things that Matt still couldn't quite understand. Takeo had a magic staff back at the apartment that Matt and Sherry had helped him set up right before they got married.

At times, Takeo felt like he didn't belong and that he would never find his place in this new world. His world had changed; it was true, but he wished he could fit in. It was such a different time period, and so many of the things around him were strange and unfamiliar. He hoped that over time, he would become accustomed to it, but Takeo's adjustment period was great.

The one thing he was good at was fighting in hand-to-hand combat. No one in any of the city precincts was able to get the better of him, even Matt, though he got a few licks in from time to time. Fighting in the way Takeo did was unlike the old-school ways that had existed in the United States for centuries. In his fighting style, too, Takeo felt like someone who didn't belong in this time. He was a warrior, over four hundred years old.

How had he acquired this ability to not age? It was just another of the things that remained unknown to him.

At the precinct one day, Takeo approached Matt in his office and shut the door gently. He was usually taciturn and judicious with his words, but when he did speak, the words he used carried weight and meaning. He spoke softly and stood calmly, waiting. He had a habit of remaining standing or moving at all times, never being seated for long; it was as if he always had some occupation close at hand. Most recently, he had helped Matt save a city from destruction.

Matt put down his pen and looked up questioningly from behind his desk.

"We must vacate New York for some time," Takeo told him in a grave tone.

"That isn't possible," Matt said.

"There are things we must go do," Takeo said. "The fate of the world depends on it."

"Someone needs to be the leader of the city," Matt protested.

With a serious look on his face, Takeo took out a piece of paper and put it on top of the desk, then stood like a statue, waiting.

Matt looked at the paper. He was rarely scared, but there were too many things he didn't understand. For instance, he didn't know the whole story about the magic of the wizards from the Temple of Time, though Takeo seemed to know much more. But Takeo had said that the survival of the world was at stake, and Matt would not ignore such a warning heedlessly. He trusted his friend implicitly.

Takeo went over to the round globe on a table in Matt's office and pointed to the intended destination.

"Why there?" Matt asked.

"Because The Master is alive. You, and only you, must come."

"What happens if The Master comes back here?" Matt asked. "How will I protect the city?"

"We were down on the dock," Takeo answered. "He isn't here in New York. We know that for a fact. God knows where he is, but he has an agenda. The fact of the matter is, this city is not under threat for the time being."

Matt got on the phone and called his crew to his office. He asked them all to take a seat. Jack, along with his new girlfriend, Lieutenant Jennifer Parker, walked in and greeted Matt. They were closely followed by Tonya and Curtis, the Triad leaders who had been very involved in fighting The Master when he attacked New York and had a vested interest in his whereabouts. The group exchanged glances. They had all begun to suspect something.

Takeo cleared his throat, as they all looked at him expectantly. He began to speak with confidence, self-assured in what had to be said at this point. Like a teacher, he began to explain his point of view, and his explanation was indeed very thorough. Passionate about the mountains in Japan, he pointed out Mount Hotaka on Matt's globe. As he went into more detail about the place where he had grown up, he said that at three thousand meters high, Mount Hotaka was one of the steepest and most dangerous mountains in Japan. How could such an incredibly tall mountain be safe at that height? The question burned in all of their eyes. Still, he and Matt needed to go there, and they needed to leave as soon as possible.

After Takeo finished going over the details, everyone had lingering questions, but he had no legitimate answers for the time being, so they all fell silent, feeling the weight of the situation settle heavy in the room.

Matt didn't know why Takeo needed to bring him, but he told the others, "There is surely a purpose. We'll find out why later, and for now, I trust him." Having the city under watch, Matt thought the timing wasn't ideal, and leaving his city would be difficult. But he told them all to work as a team, and that things would be fine. "I don't know how long we'll be. The sooner we leave, the better for everyone."

Sherry gave him a tight hug. Jack approached and gave him a clap on the back, fighting back emotion.

"I'll get what I need and come back here," Takeo said and left.

Matt agreed to that. After everyone left his office, he went home to his house in Queens to get a few things. Sherry and Jack stayed at the precinct to watch the department.

Matt and Takeo each took about an hour to prepare for their voyage. Matt had no clue regarding what he was about to embark on, but he knew without question it was a journey that would change his life. He came back to the precinct wearing warm clothes, as if he were going to Siberia. Takeo had done the same. Since New York weather was only in the high 60s in the fall, many around the precinct looked at them as as if they were nutty. But they would never dare question Matt or Takeo.

Matt requested a short meeting before they left and used it to give everyone their final instructions. Jack gave his brother a handshake and a hug. Sherry gave him a huge hug and a big kiss on the lips. Everything seemed strange to them. Takeo appeared to be trustworthy, but they wondered if they would see either of them again. Meanwhile, Sherry and the rest of them had to make Matt disappear, and how would it be possible to make a commissioner simply vanish? That was the most difficult part.

Matt and Takeo headed toward the boiler room. It was in a part of the police station that was in the back of the building. No one had gone back there for a long time. Behind a pullout piece of the wall was a stepladder. Sergeant Thomas had told Matt about it when Matt and Jack were much younger, but Matt was the only one with the key.

It was a good thing it was in a location that didn't get a lot of attention. Matt knew it was the only way to disappear. They made sure no one had followed them; then, Matt used his key to open the door, and they walked in.

Matt removed the large wooden board, the way Sergeant Thomas had shown him how to do as a kid. Takeo climbed up the ladder with the staff that he carried with him. Matt followed and grabbed the wooden board with one hand. As he stood on the ladder, he faced the wall and put the wood back in place.

The secret passage was extremely dark. Matt took out a flashlight and handed it to Takeo. "We've got about thirty steps to go," he whispered. This was a lot, for a secret passage. They both headed up the ladder to the top.

Matt explained that there would be a lock. "Just slide it from right to left, and it should open."

The lock was so rusted that Takeo broke it off with a sharp tug, then opened the old wooden door. He stepped outside and put his hands over his eyes to shield them from the bright sun.

Matt finally got to the top of the building where Takeo stood. Takeo was amazed by the city's view. He wasn't used to the buildings and had never seen anything like it. Takeo smiled. "Wait until you see what *you're* going to see," he said to Matt.

It may have been fall in New York, but Matt and Takeo, in their winter jackets, looked like Eskimos.

Takeo and Matt looked at one another. They both put their hands on the staff.

"Where did you get this?" Matt asked.

Takeo explained that the staff was magical, and that when one of the wizards had taken him back, he dropped the staff when he began to leave for wherever he was going. "I took it and kept it, just in case we ever needed it."

Matt braced himself for what he was about to experience. Even though Matt and Takeo couldn't predict what would happen, Matt was relatively certain it would not be a pleasant ride. In a way, something was terribly wrong for them to go to a place that neither one knew truly existed. Their hands grasped the staff as if their lives depended on it.

"It doesn't seem to be working," Matt said.

Just as he said that, the staff shot up with a violent jerk.

They weren't expecting such a sudden movement. As they traveled far up in the air, the staff moved faster than a plane or anything manmade. How was something so small and thin able to move so quickly? They had a great view from so high up, but it was also frightening to be thousands and thousands of feet in the air. They flew through the clouds, going up and down and from side to side. The staff flew whichever way it had to in order to avoid any collisions. It was a crazy ride, as they whizzed past planes and birds. The altitude felt amazing, and they were breathless.

Matt and Takeo were soon scared for their lives, yet exhilarated, and their hearts pounded. Neither of them had experienced anything like what they were experiencing now. The sooner they landed, the better off they would be.

Matt was afraid of heights. Takeo was usually fearless, but not being able to see the ground terrified him. Some things would scare anyone, no matter how brave. It was a hell of a ride all the way up in the sky—a ride that was reeling and furious, a journey halfway around the world, though it was a journey not yet understood by them. The only thing they knew was that it had muchy to do with the staff, the wizard, and something in between. It was a journey that they had only just begun, and a long journey at that.

They went through heavy clouds and all types of weather before finally crash-landing on top of a large hill on Mount Hotaka in Japan. It was one of the largest mountains in Japan, and it was well known to have dangerous conditions in the winter.

Takeo and Matt landed on top of some soft snow mounds. It was extremely windy and cold, and almost impossible to see. With their bags on their shoulders, they started walking, choosing each step carefully. They made sure to keep warm, never losing sight of each other. Matt followed Takeo, who knew a little about the mountains in Japan, though this wasn't the mountain where he and The Master had battled—that one was farther north.

Matt caught up with Takeo, and they walked together so they could brace themselves against the wind, but the snowy mounds stood in their way. They stopped, and the staff in Takeo's hand lit up with a strange yellow glow. Then the staff went up in the air and started turning extremely fast. As it rotated, Takeo realized it was showing the way to the secret temple. It was evident how to get there now, but getting there would prove challenging.

Takeo proceeded up the mountain, using the rope and the grappling hook he had brought with him. As they climbed in the snow, they used extreme caution, hoping to stay alive in the wintry weather. Takeo had never been on this mountain, and he tried to stay away from such dangerous mountains if he could. Matt had never been to Japan, and these last few minutes had given him good reason to stay away from any mountain.

As Matt and Takeo finally ascended the first of three large hills, they came and found themselves standing, to their dismay, in front of a group of black ninjas. Black ninjas were a secret group that worshipped ancient warriors. They knew The Master was alive, and their goal was to fight for his cause.

As the black ninjas charged at them, Matt pulled his gun out from his heavy coat. He proceeded to shoot all five of them dead where they stood.

Takeo looked at him in awe.

Matt shrugged his shoulders. "I don't want to deal with them today." Matt knew they were getting close to the temple, or something else this group didn't want them to find for some reason. He couldn't fathom why they wouldn't want the temple to be found. Matt moved the bodies aside so they didn't trip over them when they walked through the windy snowstorm.

As Matt and Takeo approached the second large mountain, they threw the rope up until it caught on something, then climbed up. This time, Matt helped Takeo. As they stood near the cliff, they heard grunting noises from behind—more black ninjas. Like true soldiers, Matt and Takeo drew out their swords in the wintry storm. The snowy conditions made them unsure of their footing, and it was difficult to move and strike. The black ninjas were equally hindered by the inclement surroundings. Matt and Takeo now knew something was surely going on, but exactly what that might be, they didn't know.

Takeo held the staff with his left hand, using it like a sword. One of the black ninjas hit the staff and it started to rumble, forcing the snow on the mountain to crumble. Matt spotted some light. Under the rocks they had been climbing over, there appeared to be a cave. What was in it, he wondered? Matt advanced, fighting the black ninjas as he moved toward the top.

The staff shook and vibrated loudly, and the hilly mountain quaked. Matt battled to get to the top of the mountain, while Takeo fought off the ninjas on the bottom. Matt pulled out his gun, but he didn't have any clear shots because of the wind. Takeo tossed a few of the black ninjas off the mountain to their swirling death.

As he began to feel the earth move, Matt took the rope off and started to twirl it as if it were a lasso. Matt had one shot, realizing the snow was tumbling, and a great big avalanche began. It was only a matter of time before it began to rumble down the entire mountain. Takeo defended himself with his sword until there was only one black ninja left near him. He seized the ninja's wrist, then fell to the ground in the snow. The black ninja saw what was happening with the snow, and Matt pulled the large warrior with all his might.

Takeo stood up and tried to pull himself with the rope and follow it to where Matt stood. The black ninjas realized what was coming. Takeo reached Matt before the avalanche hit. He still had the staff in his hand, and they both ran inside the cave. As they did, the entire mountain tumbled from above with a devastating force. It killed all the black ninjas, sending them over the mountain with a rush of cascading snow.

Matt and Takeo heard the enormous crunching noise and prayed that they wouldn't be swept away themselves. Matt knew Takeo was scared, and Takeo knew Matt was, too. They were both great fighters, but they had no control over Mother Nature. However, they were far enough into the cave that they were safe from any type of threat.

It seemed as if the rumbling of the snow lasted forever. Even when it appeared to be over, Matt and Takeo waited an extra half hour, until they knew that things were safe. As they came out of the cave, they saw that the snow had compacted against the rocks, and it was impossible to move. Takeo, with his heavy martial arts boots, gave a few kicks to a large rock. Matt joined in, and little by little, the rock began to crack. It was a monumental effort. Finally, Matt and Takeo broke the rock, and it split into two very big pieces. Some snow came through, knocking them both back. They shared a relieved laugh.

They got up and brushed the white snow off themselves. The bright sun blinded them both, and they put up their hands to shield their eyes from the light. Matt and Takeo finally got up to the top of the third and final mountain. The staff was lighting up like a Christmas tree with all sorts of colors. As Matt and Takeo helped each other to the top, they only saw mounds of snow. How was that possible? The staff had pointed to the top of the mountain. They began to wonder if they were on the right mountain. Matt hadn't been too sure. He had left that in the hands of Takeo.

Matt and Takeo looked all around. It was such a beautiful view from the top, but they wouldn't want to fall down from such a great height. They felt as if something was terribly wrong, and usually when they got a bad feeling, something bad did follow. There was supposed to be a temple. As they walked along in the snow, Takeo felt that there was something underneath that snow. It was as if they could read each other's minds. Matt understood what Takeo felt about the snow, and they both knew something was afoot. How was this temple reached? It was as if it had been buried on purpose, and no one was supposed to find it. Matt, being a police commissioner, believed things always happened for a reason. It might be a hidden reason, but it was a reason all the same. Takeo agreed that there was something not right about this. It was as if they knew something was going to happen.

Takeo used his hands to uncover a red point that stuck up out of the snow. Matt got on his hands and knees and started to dig. As they were digging, they both got hit with a snowball from behind them. There stood more black ninjas.

Matt looked at Takeo. "They just don't die, do they?"

Takeo plunged the staff deep into the snow, forcing it down so the black ninjas wouldn't get hold of it, while Matt hid from their view what Takeo was doing. For some reason, the ninjas wanted the staff, or perhaps they wanted its magic. Matt and Takeo didn't know exactly what they wanted or why.

As soon as Takeo finished, he stood up, and he and Matt drew their swords. There were twelve ninjas, dressed all in black. They stood on the mounds of snow, ready to do battle. The black ninjas had their swords drawn and ready to go as well. Matt had been practicing using his sword for months with Takeo, and he hoped he was well prepared for this moment. As the ninjas ran toward them, they began to clash swords with them. Matt and Takeo were both strong and used their strength to outmatch them. With several martial arts moves, flurries of kicks and punches, they took them out one by one, knocking them off the top of the mound and sending each one to his death. They finished the black ninjas off fairly quickly.

In minutes, the snow started to disappear and melt. As they fought the last of the ninjas, the snow dissolved from their feet, and they fell to the ground, landing on cement.

Matt and Takeo looked at the temple. "Wow!" they said in unison, highly impressed.

Takeo had heard of this temple, but never knew that

it really existed. He picked up the staff, and he and Matt walked around the temple. Matt had never seen a temple like this one. It had some odd-looking dragons on top, and there were eight equally strange-looking statues. Takeo finally realized it was the lost Temple of Time.

"Look at the top of the temple," Matt said. It had a design of red markings.

Then Takeo walked around and showed him the engraving on the doors. "Look up at the statues. Those aren't just any statues. Those are the eight wizards of time."

"The what?" Matt asked. He looked confused.

"The eight wizards of time," Takeo repeated.

"Who are they?"

Takeo continued to show Matt certain aspects of the temple, trying to make him understand the importance of this finding. He explained that the Japanese believed that this temple was created by God to watch over the world and protect the corners of the world. But an imbalance happened when the wizard was defeated and killed. "But after that, something had to happen for us to be here," Takeo said. "There must have been a disturbance in the structure. Yes, this must have been where The Master was taken. It was supposedly a place where soldiers were taken who were evil and deserved to die. This was their resting place."

"Okay, so how do we get in?" Matt asked.

Takeo picked up the magic staff.

"How about we knock?" Matt suggested.

Takeo laughed. "Like that will work," he responded.

Matt took the gold handle and hit the huge red door. The temple was large and wide, as if it housed giants. It had statues of dragons and other decorative objects on it. As the door opened slightly, Matt and Takeo had their guns by their sides. They both thought things were odd, but Takeo knew something was a lot odder than usual.

Matt didn't know much about temples, but he knew something wasn't right with the temple that had watched over the people of the world for years. Matt and Takeo walked in, and Matt thought it was strange that a temple like this had no light. Takeo knew it was odd, too. As they walked in, the door slammed closed, and the temple began to shake. It sank back into the ground from which it had come. It was a startling phenomenon.

Matt and Takeo went to a door and tried to open it. It was sealed tight, and they couldn't budge it. Matt let his instincts take over. "We were wanted here, I believe."

Takeo grinned.

Matt and Takeo took off their winter coats and moved toward the wall on one side. They were looking for a torch or something to light the temple. Takeo found a torch on the floor, and Matt found one on the wall. As they lit their torches, they saw bats hanging from the ceiling.

This wasn't like any temple that Matt had ever heard of. He looked and saw a huge fountain, perhaps similar to the Fountain of Youth. It had many fairies flying around it, and one fairy flew over to Takeo.

"You need to help them," she said. "They are all dying. The man with the gleaming skull did this."

Matt and Takeo realized she was referring to The Master, whose hair and scalp had been ripped away by Orthor.

The fairy pressed a button to intercede the traps meant

to kill intruders, and Matt and Takeo followed her through the temple's narrow passages. They finally got to a room that looked as if it belonged to the Knights of the Round Table from the days of King Arthur. The columns in the room were broken and crushed, and it was evident that there had been a battle. Matt and Takeo saw the eight wizards lying there, bleeding.

"You finally made it, Takeo and Matt," said a battered wizard, looking weak and badly hurt. It was Radagast.

"How did this happen?" Matt asked.

Radagast began to explain what had taken place. When he took The Master back to the Temple of Time, The Master magically woke up when he was locked inside this room. "Once he woke up, we saw his evil intentions. All of us threw everything we had at him, but he was too quick for any of us. He lashed out with his sword, the tip of which he had rubbed with poison, and one by one, he wounded us all."

"Poison? How in the world did he get that?" Takeo asked.

"Some Chinese guy rolled it toward him to help him."

Matt knew who he was. "Albert," he said. "When did he do this?"

"When you and Matt were otherwise occupied, he rolled him a vial of poison, and The Master hid it in his armor. When I took him, and when we landed in the temple, he rubbed the poison all over his sword, using a piece of cloth he had. Then he went into battle with us, swinging the sword and beating us all. One swing, and we all got a light brush of steel with the poison. We don't have long to live. That glass jar that stands on this broken table—the minute you came in here, it started to activate. The only way to counteract the poison is to find out what type it is. We don't have much time. Seven days from now, if you don't keep at least one of us alive, this temple will be destroyed, along with all the good in the world. The Master will have won the war. Once you leave this temple, the clock will start ticking."

"How did Nemesis fall under the control of The Master?" Matt asked.

"Do you want the long version or the short version?"

"Tell me whatever I need to know."

"Well, for starters, The Master was at your wedding."

Matt already knew that, but it was difficult for him to comprehend how The Master could return so quickly from the dead. He asked Radagast about that.

"The Master is a very powerful person," the wizard responded. "His power is unique and special. I can't tell you what he is doing or where he is, but danger is upon you and the city of New York."

"Not again!" Matt exclaimed. "How is that possible?"

Takeo and Matt kept their eyes glued to the wizard.

"We have all fought throughout time," Radagast said. "Each of us represents different time periods. All of us put together wouldn't be able to fight The Master and equal his power. He will be very difficult to stop. He is not alone in this fight. You will have great casualties—many more than before."

Matt listened intently. No matter what he and his team did, it seemed they would inevitably fall into the hands of The Master.

"The choices you make will affect you personally, Matt," the wizard said.

Matt listened more intently than ever.

"The Master will target you and affect your life more than anyone else's. Someone close to you, someone you love very much, will die. I can't tell you who, or when, but when the time comes, The Master will take someone dear. Matt, you must choose your words carefully and make your choices well."

Matt started to get angry. "Who the hell will he take from me?" he asked in a high-pitched voice.

"Matt, I can't help you any further than I already have."

"You know who it is, though, don't you?"

The wizard didn't answer. "Your focus is finding the location of The Master. You wanted to know how he got Nemesis, didn't you? Well, when he walked out of the church and you chased him down, the military vehicles were passing by. He got into the one with Nemesis. When he got back to New Jersey, Nemesis was left in the truck. Thinking the soldiers had all left, The Master got out, and as he did so, he made some noise. The soldiers shot at him, trying to protect Nemesis, but their attempt to kill The Master failed, and he slaughtered all of them. Since the garage where they were located on the base was an airtight, bulletproof room, no sound left the room.

"After every soldier was dead, The Master put all the bodies in one of the trucks and lit it on fire. He got in the truck that held Nemesis and tried to figure out how to drive it. He got the hang of it, eventually, and drove to an abandoned warehouse at Chelsea Piers. He opened the warehouse door to find a man named Albert there. Albert is the same one who threw him the poison. They connected and started to work together."

"So, Albert gave The Master the poison voluntarily?"

"Yes, he did," the wizard said. "He wanted to get back at all of those who had not believed in him. That's the sole reason he joined forces with the Master. He was greatly disappointed in everyone. It was something that had been in the works for a very long time. It just got to a point where he was willing to help. He wasn't forced."

Matt now knew that Albert had reprogrammed Nemesis.

"You have seven days to save us," Radagast warned in a somber tone. "The cure is in the haunted temple, in the Amazon."

Matt and Takeo thanked the wizard.

"Your journey will be long, my friends," he said, "but the fight you will embrace will make you stronger."

Matt and Takeo looked at each other. Things were more complicated than ever. It was virtually impossible to be in all the places they had to be at once and accomplish all the things they had to, when there was so little time. They knew they had an impossible journey to save the eight wizards and to find Nemesis. How could they ever do all of this in time?

As they shut the temple door, the hourglass began to pour. They had seven days to accomplish everything. Little time remained, and time wasn't on their side for this journey. Matt had no idea what in the world The Master wanted or where he was. That was another worry.

But for now, Matt and Takeo had to get to New York. That was their present concern.

Chapter 3

The Master, Albert, and the reprogrammed robot Nemesis were on a small boat on the water in New York City, headed out on a long journey to Romania. Albert had spent many years working on his father's dream: a time machine. With his father's sudden death due to heart failure, Albert had continued his life's work.

He had spent a lot of time on it in the past year, but he knew the time machine wasn't going to work. It needed something that he didn't understand how to create, something known as "cold fusion," a source of energy that was discovered by a scientist in Romania. The formula was stored at the Palace of the Romanian Parliament.

Then The Master showed up, and everything seemed to fall into place. With The Master as his primary ally, and the knowledge that they had full control of Nemesis, Albert now had a foolproof plan that he felt would not fail. It was a perfect plan that went along with everything that he wanted. As strange as it seemed, he and The Master had similar ideas.

The Master and Nemesis were now both under Albert's control, and it was time to execute their evil plan. Now it was off to Romania to go steal the cold fusion formula—not exactly the easiest thing to do. It would be risky, but not impossible.

By now, the world knew what The Master was capable of doing. The Master and Nemesis were far more powerful than anything the world had ever seen. The Master had made worldwide news for the destruction of New York City. Something like that gains far-reaching attention. It would be difficult for the Romanian government to try to stop them, when even the United States couldn't do it. The Master and Nemesis were two lethal weapons that seemed unstoppable, an unlikely, yet powerful pairing.

But going from New York City to Romania, and trying to get into the country from the water, seemed impossible. Albert took out his compass.

The Master, meanwhile, had many things on his mind. He wanted to get back at Matt in the worst way, but he knew things would be complex. They only had a little speedboat, and getting into international waters would be quite challenging. How would they get past so many obstacles? They didn't know much about boating, after all.

All Albert heard from The Master was complaining. It was annoying. Albert hated people who complained. He finally had enough and said, "Shut the hell up. Apparently you weren't man enough to kill Matt in the first place, or we wouldn't be in this position."

The Master grunted. "I'm going to enjoy killing you when I do."

Albert shut his mouth at that.

A smile crossed The Master's face as he put his hood back on.

The Master had set out on this journey to Romania, a far distance from New York, and he wasn't sure how they would get there. They had a large ocean to travel, with many obstacles and difficult weather conditions. Could they do it in a little speedboat?

The Master had only known Japan at a time when there was no contact with the outside world, so any other country seemed liked a lost and unfamiliar place. There were many things he would soon discover in Romania, all of its traditional European ways. The Master could not envision anything unfamiliar to him—not music, nor culture that he would find in Europe. Therefore, it seemed pointless to try to explain to him where Romania was or to show it to him on a map. The Master was one unique character, set in his own ways.

The Master knew what he wanted, and that was why Albert became so useful, but at times, he wanted to kill the old man. Albert was the brains of the outfit. He needed The Master more than he needed Nemesis, but both were valuable for the exact same reason. They were deadly, and as a team, they would be unstoppable.

Little did Albert know that once they got the energy source of cold fusion, The Master planned to go back in time, with Albert's help, and gather his warriors to help him stop Matt Rider. That was The Master's main focus—to stop Matt and kill him. He was intent on that goal. Albert was unaware of how he wouldn't stop obsessing about it until Matt was dead.

Leaning on one foot, looking out over the water, The Master seemed like the picture of a captain of a speedboat. They finally left Manhattan behind, and he waited and waited for something big to happen. He and Albert eventually fell asleep under covers that kept them from getting cold or wet from the rough waters.

They hadn't gone too far when they bumped into their first sign of trouble on the Atlantic Ocean. After a much needed rest, the rough waters woke The Master up. In the dark of the night, his red eyes were quite visible.

The crew of a large Navy aircraft carrier spotted the small boat, but at first, they didn't see anyone on it. Sensing something suspicious about this small boat, the Navy dropped anchor. They had gotten reports from Chelsea Piers about a missing boat, and this one looked similar to the description that was sent to them. Guns in hand, some of the Navy officers quietly plunged into the water, and others waited for the boat.

Still a long way from Romania, The Master and Albert slipped out of their boat into the Atlantic Ocean. They left Nemesis on the boat, uncovered, and swam toward the Navy boat. They swam underwater part of the way, thus avoiding the Navy SEALs. They reached the anchor chain, and The Master started to climb up the heavy chain first, with Albert not far behind.

Navy SEALs were trained to be quiet and careful with their movements. Gun in hand, one of the SEALs searched the boat Albert and the Master had left, while another SEAL covered him. The first SEAL removed the boat blanket, revealing Nemesis.

One of the officers realized who and what it was and radioed his captain to notify him. As he and the others watched, they all saw Nemesis awake as a demon would from a long sleep, moving its limbs and flashing its eyes. The robot took the radio from the officer, smashed the top of his skull, and killed him. The other Navy SEAL shot at him, but Nemesis grabbed the gun from the dead officer and returned fire, shooting him in the head and killing him instantly. The Navy officers shot at him with their guns, unloading round after round, but the bullets had no effect on him, since he had no flesh and was made of sturdy steel.

Nemesis stood up. He was a clear improvement over the original robot made by the military. Skinny and with a face like that of a pharaoh, he moved like a human. Albert had spent weeks upgrading Nemesis, and he was loaded with modifications. He finally came into power with his evil mind programmed into him.

The Navy men continued to unload their rounds at Nemesis, but they were no answer for him. A SEAL loaded a rocket launcher and blew up the little boat, creating a bright light that filled the sky with flames. The intense explosion alerted other ships nearby that something was terribly wrong.

As The Master and Albert finally got to the deck, Albert climbed into one of the lifeboats and pulled the top over so he could hide.

The Navy SEALs celebrated their supposed victory, thinking they had destroyed both the boat and Nemesis.

But out of the smoke from the fire came a flying pharaoh, cutting short their celebration.

The SEALs looked terrified, as the captain called for help from any nearby ships. "We are being attacked by Nemesis and The Master," he radioed. "We need help."

The overwhelming response was alarm. Meanwhile, Nemesis flew up through the fire and landed on the ship's deck. As he landed, the Navy sailors backed up toward the planes. The Master then appeared out of nowhere.

The captain sounded the ship's alarm. "All hands on deck. The Master and Nemesis are on the ship," he said over the loudspeaker.

The sleeping sailors in the cabin got dressed as quickly as possible. Women and men ran and grabbed any weapon from the ship they could, whatever they could get their hands on. The sailors started to battle and ran from Nemesis toward The Master. They trembled, facing two of the most unstoppable forces that the world had ever seen.

Nemesis flew right up to the large guns on the ship and melted them with a fiery blowtorch in mere seconds. Then Nemesis flew back down to watch The Master do battle. The Master stood on the aircraft carrier with seamen shooting at him. Shocked, they watched as bullet after bullet bounced off of him. They had never seen anything like this resilience.

Seamen came running from every which way, with guns in their hands. The Master stood by himself, slashing at anything that moved, dropping body after body. Many fought him, but none were successful against him.

Nemesis then turned his attention to one of the planes. He put his palm forward, and a large, destructive ray emitted from his hand, blowing up the plane. One by one, Nemesis destroyed each of the planes on the aircraft carrier. The explosions lit up the sky.

Still hiding, Albert peeked out from under the cover on the boat. He was terrified. He had never seen such destruction from two beings. He particularly watched The Master in awe. He was a force that he didn't think even Nemesis would be able to stop. The Master's quickness was unique. Albert couldn't remember seeing anyone with such agility and strength. It was as if he were a ghost, leaving a death trail behind him.

More seamen ran toward The Master, and Nemesis had his own seamen to deal with as well. A robot or human: which would most choose if they had the option?

The battle intensified as seamen from the bottom of the ship eventually made their way up to the top. As more came, more dropped. It was a sight to see how The Master was too strong even for a numbers game. He struck many with his hands and feet, then used his swords to finish the job. He killed many, and no one gave The Master any real fight. There were no ships in the near distance that would be able to reach them in time to help.

As for Nemesis, his prowess was also impressive. He used his functions as a robot, and his punches sent a variety of sailors across the ship. Sometimes, he launched them in the air so high that by the time they landed, they were already dead on impact. His guns and other weapons were just as lethal. The seamen shot at him, but Nemesis's hands were like The Master's. He was able to block anyone from trying to stop him just as easily as The Master did. It wasn't easy to contend with either one of them.

Albert poked his head out from time to time, realizing he had two of the most indestructible weapons at his disposal. The Master was more than that—he was a walking weapon. His skull was intimidating, and something about those red eyes always instilled fear. What would happen if they succeeded in what they planned? They were still far from Matt; yet, they were able to walk over everyone who stood in their way. As the hours passed, bodies lay everywhere, and the number of living sailors became fewer and fewer. Nemesis had killed many very easily, and The Master's body count was very high. But the two of them still stood tall.

The Navy vessel looked just as bad as if it had been in any war the U.S. had ever fought, from the destroyed planes to the fires still noticeable in the night sky. It was one of the worst attacks against the Navy ever. How could this have happened?

What would Matt do? He still had a journey of his own to complete.

The Master killed one of the last seamen, and bodies lay everywhere. The top of the ship looked like a battlefield. The Master had a slight smile on his face. It had been a good fight.

Albert watched as the bloodied bodies remained motionless. He decided it was time to climb out of the boat.

The Master's sword was covered in blood, as was the rest of him, including his skull. As he walked toward Nemesis, he left a trail of blood behind him. Three seamen stood in front of Nemesis, who punched one, knocking his head off cleanly. He threw another overboard, and he ripped off the third's arm and jammed the arm down his throat. Both The Master and Nemesis were vicious and destructive.

The ship was still anchored, and its main level was all red, as if someone had painted the deck. Albert approached The Master and pointed to the tower where he thought the captain was hiding. The Master tried the door to the tower, but it was locked from the inside. Nemesis grabbed the door, ripped it off its hinges, and threw it off the ship. The Master walked in, and it looked like a construction site, things hanging all over the place. A seaman came running, and Nemesis grabbed one end of an iron piece that was held by wires. With great force, he pushed it toward the seaman and hit him with it as he was walking up the stairs. It went through his stomach, killing him. The blood dripped down through the stairs and the other wires that hung. It was a mess.

The Master headed upstairs, while Nemesis and Albert went downstairs. The Master had drawn his sword, but he sheathed it. The ship was large, and there were many things to check. He knew that there were other seamen around. As he got up the stairway, he saw many doors down the corridor, each made of metal. They all looked similar to each other.

Sparks flew off the ceiling lights, which had been flickering. The Master had to cover his red eyes to keep from getting hurt. He wasn't scared at all. He loved being this type of warrior. He had never been on a ship before and didn't quite know what to expect. It didn't seem like anything special, being inside a Navy ship. He knew one thing: anything that walked had to die—except for the captain. The Master knew he couldn't kill the captain of the ship, because he was the only one who knew how to get to Romania. The Master and Albert had no idea, and Nemesis had been programmed to be a war machine, not a navigational tool.

The Master moved the wiring aside that had fallen. He walked cautiously, knowing he might run into other seamen. He went from room to room and opened each door, looking for any other seamen who might want to kill him. One or two of the rooms had a few seamen alive inside. The Master used his hands and feet to kill them, bringing the body count higher for his tally. He was an unstoppable machine. The nearer he came to the end of the corridor, the more seamen came out. He calculated that the soldiers were hiding and protecting the captain. Smoke from the open ceiling tiles blocked his vision.

The Master finally got near the end of the corridor, with only two rooms remaining. One room had a huge door, and the other had two doors. The Master stood in front of the room with the two doors and opened one of them. The room looked as if it were decorated for a party. Tables were set for a dinner banquet, and equipment had been set up for a DJ. A sign on the wall read: "Happy 50th Birthday, Captain!" The Master walked in, and under the many tables were seamen ready to defend the captain.

As soon as they heard the door shut, four seamen ran the captain to the ship's bridge. Once the door shut from behind them, The Master turned around and saw no one. He tried to open the door, but it had an electronic lock and wouldn't budge. The Master took his sword out and hit the lock with powerful swings, only leaving scratch marks on the lock. The Master then heard noises from around the room. He had his swords already drawn. He was a warrior with great instincts, and he sensed that something wasn't right.

As he got closer and closer to the stage, he began to hear movement. The smoke machine had been left on, and the smoke hurt The Master's eyes so that he had to keep rubbing them. When he reached the tables set up near the stage, the lights dimmed and turned off. He heard rattling noises as seamen and Navy officers came out from under the tables, and plates, beer mugs, and wine glasses crashed to the floor.

Unable to see, The Master dropped his swords and fell to one knee. The men all wore masks to protect their eyes and to help them breathe. They had formed a plan and outsmarted him with the smoke, and they had him where they wanted him. Who would have thought something so simple would work? One of the stronger men, a Navy officer, came running from behind and threw a heavy chain around The Master's chest.

The Master had no idea what had happened. He was on his knees, and he couldn't breathe. The officer kicked away his swords so he couldn't reach them, and then finished wrapping the chain around the weakened warrior. He was down and out, knocked out cold by the incapacitating gas in the ventilation system.

After a few minutes, one of the officers turned off the system, and The Master was gagged and carried out of the room. His arms were wrapped tightly, and he couldn't move. As the Navy officers dragged him outside, the wind whistled in the night, and the breeze woke him up. He struggled to move, but with a secure lock on the chain, there was no way he could get free. The expression on his face showed that he knew that he wasn't getting out of the chains. He spat out angry words in his own language. He had been caught off guard, and he knew it.

The officers walked to the edge of the ship, nudged him over, and pushed him into the Atlantic Ocean. He began to sink, all the while trying to use his strong shoulders to somehow force the chains off of him.

The Navy officers had finally gotten rid of The Master. They thought they had killed him, but one officer stood watching the ocean. There was something about The Master that made it seem impossible for him to die.

The Master sank quickly with the weight of the chains around him and hit the bottom of the ocean. He struggled to get the chains off, rubbing his back against some of the rocks on the ocean floor, trying to chip away at the chains. Several minutes after sinking to the bottom, his great power and strength prevailed, and he finally got the chains to snap.

The Navy had gotten the better of him, but so what? He got wet and went for a nice swim. He had pretty much enjoyed it. He laughed to himself.

The Master swam up to the surface, grabbed on to the anchor chain, and climbed up. He stood up, dripping from head to toe, angry and seeking revenge. He saw the men walking away across the deck. "You didn't kill me," he said. "Just try to bring it. You are pitiful."

The Master drew his sword and ran toward them, swinging at the Navy men and disemboweling them in a matter of minutes. They'd had no chance. The Master then took his sword, and even though each of them was dead, he swung at their heads and cut them off, leaving them all decapitated. They had really pissed him off.

The Master took off toward the tower where Nemesis and Albert Herr were heading. He saw with his beady red eyes that the captain was also hiding in the tower. The Master knew not to take the metal doors leading into the ship's upper deck and lower deck. There was heavy thunder and lightning this particular night, and the water was choppy.

The Master ran toward an opening on the ship where he could climb up to get to the captain. He took his time, as a few men watched for any light, which was very limited because of how many things had been destroyed during the battle. So, the Master timed the lightning strikes to his pursuit and ran to a safe spot where he then counted every ten seconds, making sure he kept out of sight. With the heavy gusts of winds and rain, it was virtually impossible to see on the deck of the ship. The Master crept up little by little, taking it slow. The storm made it difficult at times to run and hold on without falling. He wanted to take his time. The ship wasn't going anywhere.

The Master finally got to a spot directly under the communication center, a place where he couldn't be seen. As he was about to climb up, the door swung open and three guards shot their guns, hitting the Master and blowing him backward into large water puddles. The rain made it difficult for the soldiers to see, and blowing him off his feet hadn't been the smartest idea, either.

It was hard to see anything with the wind and downpour, and The Master used this to his advantage. He threw crates to blindside them and knocked the three guards down to the ground. The Master jumped onto a few of the crates that stood in front of him, gaining height, and leaped off the crates with his sword in hand. He landed on the first guard, gashing the right side of his face and killing him instantly. He used his sword on the second one, gouging it through his stomach, and then he put his sword through the third man's chest. The Master pulled the sword out of his last victim, and then used the door frame as leverage to climb up the wet door.

The Master was very agile and could leap where not many others could. With it being so wet, it was hard to keep his grip. The Master didn't want to fall. He had planned to climb up the side of the tower to the top and cut all power. But realizing that destroying the ship's power wouldn't get them to Romania, he changed his plans. He saw a crack in a small window and in a swift motion, he kicked the window, shattering it. The Master then climbed through the broken glass.

The Master stood in the hallway and saw the broken pieces of the wall. Nemesis and Albert had found the captain, and Nemesis had thrown two of the Navy men through the wall, creating a huge hole. The pharaoh-like robot was very strong, possibly an even match for The Master, and he had more weapons with which to kill.

The entire ship's crew had been killed. Nobody was left except the captain, who lay on the floor. The Master and Nemesis were two killing machines. It would have been hard to stop one of them, let alone the two. Whatever they wanted to do, they surely could do.

Nemesis carried the captain out of the room. Surrounded by The Master and Albert, the captain looked terrified. With his beady red eyes that made him look as if he were from hell, the Master gave him an evil grin that suggested the captain's voyage was his last—and it might well be. The captain knew that without a crew on the ship, he was the only one who could drive the boat. But when they got to Romania, he believed he would surely be killed as the rest of the crew had been. It was scary. Just seeing what they were able to do in a short amount of time was unbelievable.

The Master drew his sword to the captain's throat and looked into his eyes. "If you run, I will kill you," he said. The Master smiled fiendishly. In his mind, he was hoping that he would. The Master put down his sword, and they headed into the captain's quarters. His long battle had made The Master fatigued. Everyone else was weary, too.

Nemesis carried the captain to his chair at the helm. Albert lay on the couch, and The Master sat back in another chair. The captain pressed the computer buttons to operate the ship, and they began their journey to Romania. Their trip through the Atlantic Ocean would be a long one. The storm continued, and as the boat shifted in the rough waters, some dead bodies fell off the deck and landed in the water. Bad storms were common in those waters.

With his black unfeeling eyes, Nemesis followed the captain's every move. As a war machine that Albert had created, Nemesis was well programmed not to fail in his mission. The robot was one of the few of Albert's reprogrammed machines that had finally turned out the way he wanted. Nemesis would have his day of reckoning come to fruition very soon.

~~~
~~~

Two days had passed, and back in New York, a trail of dead bodies had been discovered and called in to the local police station. Sherry and Jack took another drive down to Chelsea Piers. As they pulled up, they mused that another visit seemed too soon, since they had been there only a few days ago. The same sweet old man greeted them, but the police had search parties in the water, and dead bodies were all lined up on the pier.

Sherry was shocked.

Jack looked at the ships in the water. "Where's the Navy ship?" he asked. "Usually it's stationed here." He directed his speech to the old man and asked for the log of the ships.

"It's the Navy," the man said. "They don't need to be told where they can go."

"How the hell did he take out the entire Navy ship?" Jack asked.

Sherry shrugged her shoulders. It was mind-boggling.

The water was filled with boats and police divers bringing up body after body, along with the Coast Guard trying to locate the ship. The Navy ship they were looking for was well out of New York, and could have been headed anywhere by now. It was impossible to find.

Sherry now knew how Matt had felt. She was beginning to get aggravated.

Seeing that look on her face, Jack said, "You remind me of my brother when you look like that." He laughed.

Not the type to be mocked, Sherry gave him a dirty look. "Let's go," she said.

As they walked down Chelsea Piers, there had to have been hundreds of bodies that had been pulled out of the water, along with the boats that were out in the Atlantic Ocean. Once the bodies had been reported, the Coast Guard had ordered the boats originally in the water to leave as soon as possible. Due to the storm, there hadn't been many.

Sherry had no way of getting in contact with Matt in Japan, and knew he would be in for a rude awakening when he came back. It was unfortunate. Matt was trying to save the eight wizards of the world. He had no idea what was going on worlds away. When he came back, his own world would be turned upside-down.

~~~

Nemesis watched all day and all night on the journey to a place far away from New York. Nemesis and Albert had so much planned, and they knew what it was going to take: a lot of hard work and determination.
~~~

Chapter 4

As the Navy vessel finally reached port and dropped anchor far from New York, the captain had known that his death was imminent. But neither The Master nor Nemesis had to do anything. The captain's stress was ultimately his downfall. He had a heart attack and died from it.

How they had gotten by all the foreign ships in the water was curious, but timing had everything to do with it. The Master, Albert, and Nemesis had to get off the Navy ship without being noticed. Some dead bodies remained on the ship's runway, which were hard to miss.

They had one intention—to get to the Palace of the Romanian Parliament and get the cold fusion formula that the Romanian president kept in a secure location. They had one boat that wasn't totally destroyed. They went to the back of the ship and lowered the speedboat into the water. Nemesis kept on the lookout, watching every move of anyone in the waters. As the boat was lowered, he and Albert went down the unstable ladder. After they got down to the boat and left in it, The Master turned around to see many officers surrounding him with their AK-47s and other high-powered weapons pointing right at him.

It was cold, and being near the water produced more than chills down the spine. The people of Romania had no idea what had gone on in New York, so when they saw a man with swords, body armor, and an exposed skull, they thought it was a joke and laughed.

The Master had his sword in hand and didn't put it down, though the officers asked him several times to drop the weapon. As early dusk set in, they began to look up at the sky, as if searching for something. The Master noticed this and took advantage of the situation. With his swords, he went at the ten men there to arrest him. They responded with their guns, making a very loud noise.

The gunshots echoed in the air, signifying trouble. Nemesis and Albert, who had docked their boat farther down the pier, could hear the sounds. The Master went at the soldiers, using both of his swords, slicing the guns' muzzles right off. After a while, he put his swords away and began to use his high-powered punches and mighty kicks as if he needed a slight workout from the soldiers. He broke ribs and caused injuries that would have lasting, damaging effects. As he finally disposed of them all, he dived headfirst into the Black Sea. Time wasn't on their side.

Albert began to look up at the sky. He knew who Dracula was—a fictional character he didn't actually believe in. But the soldiers started to give him more reason to believe.

The Master swam toward the boat to join Nemesis and Albert. He climbed aboard and put on his monk-like garments. It almost seemed as if he were pretending to worship and acting as if he belonged more than he did. It was hard to believe that they had finally made it to a place so far away from home.

Both Albert and The Master noticed the heavy clouds filling the sky. It was getting extremely dark. They thought it odd that no one seemed to care that they were there, although some realized who they were from television reports.

One man came running up to them. "You must run," he warned. "It is nearing night, and the Count is hungry."

"Who is this Count?" The Master asked.

Albert began to explain, "Count Dracula. He's a vampire, and he feasts on human blood in order to survive."

The Master's eyes lit up. The Master had no idea what a vampire was or how to kill one, but that didn't matter. It presented a new challenge. "I want to meet him, so I can kill him," he said.

Albert knew he was serious. Some of the people on the pier looked at the Master speculatively. They thought that if anyone had a shot at killing Dracula, it would be him. But no one stopped to have a conversation with him.

A lot of the boats were back in port. They all tried to get back before sundown. Albert was scared already and wouldn't continue. He wanted to find a hotel where he would be safe.

The old pier was unique and fresh-looking, as if it had just been built, though it hadn't. The Master walked past a lot of factories and other businesses. From where he stood, he looked across the horizon and saw a tall castle that reached to the sky. It wasn't like any castle he had ever seen. From a distance, it looked perfect and neatly kept.

The Master was guided up a set of stairs that led out of the pier. On each side of the stairs were buildings that, though old, were intact. The Master knew that they were old, but he didn't know just how old. He noticed the clothes hanging on clotheslines. The people didn't seem to have much money, so they did things to help save.

As The Master finally reached the top, an old man with a cane and a long white beard struggled to stand. He courageously greeted the Master and handed him a map.

The Master opened it up and looked at it. The old, crusted paper seemed like the same kind of paper that the scrolls from The Master's past were written on. The Master saw that it was a map of Dracula's castle. He rolled it back up and thanked the man. The Master was being kinder and more patient than usual. It was strange and very out of the ordinary. The Master heard a screeching noise.

"He is coming," the old man said.

The Master grabbed the old man, and at the first place that looked safe, he opened the door and put him down. As The Master walked outside, he saw a large mutant bat-like creature in the dark sky, flying around as if it were waiting for prey. Whatever it was must have spotted the Master with the old man, and it knew the old man was vulnerable. The big monster was around six feet tall, all black, and had a medallion around its neck and sharp claws on its hands and feet. Its ears were pointy, and its nails were even longer.

The Master spotted a ladder not too far away. It apparently had been used for some construction on one of the other buildings. The Master climbed up the ladder and saw the old man sitting in a rocking chair in front of the fire, rosary beads in his hands. As he prayed, his scared dog whimpered at his side.

As the bat dived down toward The Master, The Master drew his sword and fended it off. It was ironic that it was that house near the pier that he seemed to be so focused on. The Master finally got to the top of the old man's house. He stood and watched with his red eyes that seemed to light up the sky and made him very noticeable wherever he was.

The bat dived at The Master again and tried using its claws to hurt him. The Master ducked. He had a feeling this was going to be quite a battle. He moved to different sides of the roof, listening for the bat's call. As the bat dived toward The Master one last time, The Master jumped as high as he could, cutting the bat with his fifteen-and-a-half-inch katana blade. He caught it right in the stomach, causing it to crash and fall down over a few buildings and land in the Black Sea.

The Master stood on top of the building and couldn't determine where the bat had landed. He climbed back down the ladder and saw the old man standing outside his house. It was as if the old man knew who he was, and something about him brought back a memory from the distant past.

"Remember, my son," the old man said, "use a wooden stake and hit his heart with it."

Why a stake? The Master wondered. *I will use my sword.* The Master walked along the pier using his warrior's instinct. Trying to hide was very hard. His eyes always gave him away. As the bat approached, The Master's eyes lit up and fire came out, igniting the bat and causing it to crash down onto the street. This was an ability of his that had rarely been seen.

In hundreds of years, Dracula himself had never seen

anyone like this. He rolled on the ground, and the fire extinguished. Dracula glared at the Master in anger. He knew he wasn't human, or if he was, he was stronger than anyone else who had ever tried to kill him.

The Master had his sword in his hand, dripping with Dracula's blood. As The Master walked toward him, Dracula turned back into the bat again and flew straight at The Master, sending him so far up in the air that it seemed like miles. The Master came crashing down on a hay wagon, shattering it to pieces.

Bleeding badly, the bat held its stomach. A loud noise came out of its large snout. The Master slowly came around, but the bat never flew to see whether The Master was dead.

The Master broke a piece of wood from the wagon in half. One piece he held, and the other, he put aside. The Master stood up and sneakily went from house to house, hiding under the aprons that overlapped the building. As the bat took off toward the castle, it saw The Master was gone. The bat's cry grew greater and greater.

The Master was only a few feet away, hiding. He closed his eyes. It was the only way to keep the bat from spotting him. Then he came out from the side of the building apron he was hiding under, jumped onto the bat's wings, and grabbed it. The bat flew up in the air as The Master repeatedly punched it in the chest, causing more and more blood to spurt. The bat tried to reach The Master with its claws and sharp nails. With his right hand, The Master grabbed its claws, and with his left, he used the piece of wood to stab the bat in the wing on its left side, causing the bat to fall. The bat tumbled into a construction site where vehicles were parked. The Master also fell and crashed through the skylight of a bed warehouse, shattering all the glass and landing on a mattress.

The bat was getting irate. The Master had messed him up more than anyone in history. Van Helsing had never given Dracula the punishment that The Master had given him. Now in human form, Dracula got up. He was hurting, but not enough to keep him from coming back for more.

The wind started to pick up speed, making it hard to walk. It blew the doors off the factory building that The Master occupied. As Dracula stood in the doorway, he started to spin round and round like a missile and went hurtling toward The Master. The Master grabbed his knife with his right hand and fell back so that Dracula missed him. But The Master didn't miss Dracula. Timing his move perfectly, he plunged a knife into Dracula's upper chest. The Master landed the blow with a strong motion from his hand, causing Dracula to crash directly into the wall. Dracula's white shirt was covered in blood.

The Master got to his feet first and took out his sword. Dracula pulled the knife out and lay there in pain. "How could a human being do this to me? I am the dark prince. I can't die," he hissed.

The Master approached Dracula and kicked him in the head as he lay there, nailing him with the spikes on his boot, causing his head to bleed. There wasn't one place on his body that The Master hadn't weakened.

To Dracula's shock, The Master picked him up quite easily and ran with him, hitting column after column, splitting the thick wood into pieces. He finished by brutally throwing Dracula right through the last one. Dracula was hurting badly. The Master relentlessly knelt on top of him and straddled him with both legs. With the spikes in his gloved hands, The Master bloodied Dracula more and more with each vicious punch. The Master picked his head up and punched his face, rearranging it to the point that he was unrecognizable through the blood that covered him.

Dracula lay on the ground in a pool of his own blood. The Master leaned over and saw the medallion that from generation to generation had meant so much to the Prince of Darkness. He ripped it off Dracula's neck and began to crumple it up as if it were a piece of paper. The Master dropped the medallion and left Dracula there in the warehouse. He went outside, and with all his strength, pushed the building over, separating it from its loose foundation. The entire building came crashing down right on top of Dracula.

The people watching from their windows were amazed. How was The Master so much stronger than Dracula? They never would have imagined this to be possible. They were shocked that of all people, a Japanese warrior had beaten the hell out of Dracula.

The Master walked away from the crumbled building that lay destroyed on the pier. The old man was in shock as well. If anyone had bets on it, the underdog would have been The Master, but that was not the case whatsoever.

The Master wondered what was so special about this figure. He wasn't evil—he was a wimp, he scoffed to himself. The Master had fought tougher men. Even Matt Rider seemed a lot tougher to him in that moment. Perhaps Dracula had never faced such a worthy opponent because most people would never challenge him out of fear of what might happen to them if they tried.

The Master had a far journey now. He had killed Dracula, and that was step one. Now he wanted to get to the castle to explore what was in it. He thanked the old man.

The old man looked at him. "Beware of the Prince of Darkness," he said. "Be warned that he might not be dead if you didn't stab him with a wooden stake through his heart."

"This doesn't matter. Either way, I can't be killed," The Master told him. "It is time for me to head to the castle. I will destroy everything in that damn castle, until his name is gone from anything he ever owned. If he is not dead, then he'll wish that he was."

The Master started to walk toward the castle, which seemed miles upon miles away. It was still nighttime, but some light started to appear. A loud cry echoed on the pier.

In disbelief at what he had heard, The Master turned his head to look, then went back down the stairs, pacing himself carefully. The people began to see and hear movement among the rocks.

The Master finally got down to the destroyed building. He went over and heard the cries and saw the rocks begin to move. To his dismay, he saw the feet. Dracula was alive. He couldn't believe it. The creature came shooting out of the rocks with the force of thunder and flew over him. With an annoying cry, it looked at him and stuck up its middle claw, then took off. The Master knew Dracula was hurting and had gone off to regroup. The Master had punished him enough, and he wasn't able to wage a return attack on The Master.

It was true that the fight had been taken out of Dracula. No one previously had fought Dracula and won, but The Master had fought him and beat the hell out of him. The

Master wasn't afraid of anything, nor should he have been. He was stronger than Dracula and possessed a mighty power that no one had seen before.

The morning came quickly. It was time for The Master to start his journey toward the castle.

The old man came out to view the damage and destruction to the pier. He bid goodbye to The Master. The Master, after the events of the night before, was looked upon as a god, and that he was in many ways. He began to hear cheers, something he wasn't used to. In a way, he was doing them all a favor. The Prince of Darkness was evil and had taken many lives in the old village of Transylvania, an area The Master now had as his destination. Transylvania was a historical region in the central part of Romania, bounded on the east and the south by the Carpathian Mountains, which could be seen anywhere near Transylvania.

The village was bound by its old-school European style. The medieval town was known for its nine towers, narrow passageways, cobbled streets, burgher houses, and old churches. The town was nothing like anything The Master had ever seen. Even old-school Japan wasn't anything like this. It was so nice that he never even thought to destroy any of the beautiful buildings. The mountains stood out, day or night, and the beauty of the scenery left The Master speechless. Though it seemed hard to imagine, it gave him a great feeling.

As The Master walked through the town, he noticed that even with his evil skull, the people were not afraid of him. Perhaps that was understandable because they had to deal with Dracula, who was equally hideous, if not more so. The village looked peaceful, though it was disturbed at times by this monster. A number of shops were set up where merchants sold different things, from Romanian styles and perfumes to food and drink. The Master had never seen anything like this before.

He felt at times that what he was doing was wrong, but he had never asked for his own parents to be killed coming off the mountain. He had to get revenge on the wizard and other people who got in his way. Similarly, these villagers had never asked Dracula's wrath to rain down on them and for the monster to use them at feeding time.

The Master learned a lot from the old man and from the people of the village. For once, the skull and his red eyes did not induce fear at the sight of him. No one was afraid of him. He felt at peace. But he wasn't being told what to do. It was his decision to help, something he wanted to do. This brought him a sense of purpose.

He felt he knew the old man from a distant past, and he was someone who had a heart, as if he were trying to help The Master. The old man believed in him when most didn't. No one had ever believed in him, and here was a man at the pier who talked to him and showed no fear at all. It made the warrior's smile shine out through his skull.

As he strolled around the rest of the village, an old lady who saw him walking by came out of her house. "Come in, my son," she said. "You will need your rest."

He went into her house and put down his sword and belt. The Master never trusted anyone, but the old man had trusted him, and the old woman gave him food and sheltered him so he could rest. She made him tea—a special tea for battered warriors—which he drank gratefully. She led the way to a spare bedroom, decorated in a European style. He lay down, shut his eyes, and rested.

The old woman rubbed his skull. "When it is time, you will awaken from your sleep," she said.

The afternoon passed, and he slept. When The Master woke up, it was as if he were a new warrior.

The old woman saw that he was up. The old man was in the house, and the woman explained, "We have been married for fifty years, and we know everyone and everything. We know things about you that most wouldn't understand. When you kill Dracula, we will help guide you to become the person who you truly are. You have good in you, and we want you to find it. It is time for your fight."

The Master, empowered by these words, left and went toward the castle.

Chapter 5

The old man and woman watched the fearsome warrior head toward the large castle situated in a wooded area. The Master had spent a lot of time with them. It gave him a new outlook after four hundred years, and his time spent with the kind old couple helped him realize how to go about killing Dracula, who was a lot younger than he was.

The Master walked through the wooded area as many watched from their houses. They knew that he was their only hope for living a normal life. The old couple knew he was destined for great things and had faith that he would do what was needed. Already he had done things that no human—not even Van Helsing—had done to Dracula over the years. The Master could not be killed; nor could Dracula, except in a particular way. The old man and woman had told The Master how to kill him, and gave him a stake to use.

Just before he left their house, The Master had said, "I am going to rip Dracula's heart out and kill him."

As the darkness rose and noises from the castle began

to grow louder and louder, the only light was the red light from The Master's eyes. It was a sore point with The Master, because it meant that Dracula might detect his whereabouts.

It was The Master's intent to kill Dracula, and he knew Dracula was out to get him as well. The Prince had never gotten so brutally manhandled before. He had never been the one to leave the fight without winning until now.

The Master was ready. As he approached a darkened graveyard, he saw zombies come out of the graves. He knew it was a plot orchestrated by Dracula to have him killed. The Master made very light work of killing all of them with his sword. It was not a fair battle.

Dracula watched from one of the trees, and he knew that he was in for more than his share of fighting as well.

A pack of wolves appeared and attacked The Master. They knocked him down, biting at him, but never getting a grip on any part of him. The Master grabbed one of the wolves, snapped its neck, and threw it off him. He used his red eyes to roast another one and reduce it to mere bones.

Dracula knew most of the wolves wouldn't survive. He started to doubt himself. *How can I stop a man who simply does not stop?* he thought, flying back to his castle.

The Master knew Dracula had watched him in the graveyard. He stepped over the zombies' limbs and the dead wolves. The grass and the ivy that hung from the old gates gave him the feeling that he was approaching something of ancient evil. That didn't scare The Master, even though he wasn't used to this type of fight. His battles had all been on the battlefield, not against a being who wasn't human. But as in any contest, he would have to figure out his opponent's weakness.

The reddish-white castle was one of the largest castles in the region, if not the largest, and not hard to find. It stood alone, surrounded by many trees and bushes. It had many different red-and-white peaks that had been well maintained through the years, and not too many windows, for an obvious reason: Dracula hated sunlight.

The Master swung open the rusted gate and broke it off with a strong push. He walked across a drawbridge, like those of most of the old castles, and continued walking along the side of the castle, by some trees. When he put his arms out to his side and closed his eyes, his body lifted up, and he slipped through an open window and landed inside Dracula's castle.

The Master entered the darkened castle on guard with his two swords in hand, ready for anything and everything. His bright skull lit up, and he was the only source of light in the eerie surroundings. He looked around at the rugs, the furniture, the china, and the unique paintings. They all appeared priceless and would delight any collector. Everything had the look of the medieval period and represented that era very well. It was almost as if the castle itself were an antique, and in a way, it was.

The old man had given The Master a map of the castle, but no one other than Van Helsing had ever seen the inside. Many hadn't survived their battle against Dracula, and his legend in Transylvania continued to grow.

Meanwhile, word had traveled throughout Europe and Asia and had gotten back to the United States that The Master was fighting Dracula. Sherry and Jack happened to catch the story on the news while at work. They saw it in

Matt's office on his iPhone. They almost had heart attacks when they saw the footage. They couldn't believe what they had seen.

Back in the castle, The Master looked for light switches along the wall, but only found unlit candles. From the look of the cobwebs around the room, no one had been in this room for decades. With his red eyes, The Master tried to locate a circuit breaker and found one behind two large knights. He had a sinking suspicion that they were alive, and he knew not to trust anything he saw.

The room was very high, with stairs going up three flights. Dracula looked down from above, watching as the knights came alive just as The Master had predicted. With their spears in hand, they charged The Master in their metal suits. The Master did a few backflips in the open space, then put his hands together and didn't move as the knights grew closer and closer to him. The Master then sent forth a power source from his hands that shattered both knights, blowing them to pieces and vaporizing them instantaneously.

Dracula shielded himself from the explosions. Nothing he threw at The Master stopped him. He was an impossible force that was still walking and breathing.

The Master saw something that made him think the room concealed a secret passage, so he pressed along the wall and found a switch near the bookcase. Dracula seemed suspicious. Not many knew of that passage. It was where only the Wolfman walked through the castle. He was locked up in a cage and was controlled by Dracula. He steeled himself, realizing that it was time that he proved his loyalty.

A full moon had come up, and The Master heard what

sounded like a wolf. It was the Wolfman. The ferocious, ravishing Wolfman leaped at the Master, sending him flying. The Wolfman looked up at Dracula, and Dracula indicated he wanted The Master dead through a silent signal. The Master got up without his swords and stood in position, waiting for the Wolfman to attack him. From under the armor on his forearm came two long blades. As the Wolfman jumped at him with his large, imposing figure, The Master took advantage of the ample body of the creature and embedded the two knives in the Wolfman's chest. The Master ripped them out of his chest, grabbed the Wolfman's legs, and twirled him around and around, sending him right through the thick wooden drawbridge.

The Master walked with authority. Dracula was shocked at his strength and power. The Wolfman was hurt, and he saw The Master coming. He leaped and swung at him with his sharp claws, knocking The Master away from him. Dazed from the hit, The Master lay on the ground. When the Wolfman leaped at him again, the Master lifted his legs and threw the Wolfman into a tree.

The Master got up again, staggering. As he did, spikes extended out on top of both of his hands. He grabbed the Wolfman and repeatedly punched him with the spiked hands. Bleeding from the punches, the Wolfman ran toward The Master and bit his armor, cracking his sharp fangs and eventually breaking them.

The Master pushed him off and jumped at him, hitting his snout with a powerful punch and breaking his jaw. The Wolfman leaped at him, as he had no line of defense anymore. He started clawing at him, but did little damage to The Master's armor. Then the Wolfman punched The Master and sent him crashing through a log, breaking it into two big pieces. The Master held one piece in his hand. The Wolfman leaped at The Master, and the Master swung at him, using the log like a baseball bat. He sent the Wolfman flying what seemed like miles away, through all the trees that were in his path. Hearing trees come crashing down with the thunderous impact of the beast, The Master threw the log down and went after him. The Wolfman lay hurt and unconscious.

Attempting to be stealthy, the Master quietly climbed up in a tree and jumped from one tree to another. Scouting the Wolfman out, he came closer and closer, until he finally found him. With two knives in his hands, The Master waited patiently for the Wolfman to get up, which took some time. He was hurt from the impact, and his broken jaw had silenced him so that Dracula couldn't locate him by his cry.

The Master saw him finally getting up, as he hid under the cover of tree branches. With the Wolfman's back turned toward The Master, he leaped with both knives in his hands and nailed him in both shoulders at once. The Wolfman had little roar left in him as his mouth opened and blood came gushing out. The Master gave him a powerful kick in the face and a punch to the animal's gut, with a crushing blow that cracked three of his ribs. The Master backed away and gave him a side kick, sending him through the air. He landed on a vine bush full of thorns.

The Master grabbed the Wolfman's neck with a tight grip and began to squeeze until he couldn't breathe. The Wolfman began to struggle, and his feet writhed and kicked, but The Master was too powerful for him. When The Master heard his neck snap, he dropped him and walked away.

But the old couple had made sure he knew that to kill the Wolfman, he must use a silver bullet. The Master had a gun that the old man had taught him how to use. The Wolfman got up and quickly knocked the gun out of The Master's hands to prevent himself from getting killed.

The Master was furious. His eyes grew red, and as the Wolfman went to attack him, fireballs came out of The Master's eyes and lit the Wolfman on fire. The Wolfman ran toward the castle to get to the water and extinguish the fire. Before he could get there, The Master stuck out his hands on each side of his chest, and electrical power came out of each hand. The Wolfman backed away from him. The Master had an electrical power source and used it as a whip that caught the Wolfman. The Master's eyes were possessed, and he was a powerful weapon.

Dracula got his ladies to come and get ready for him. He was next on The Master's list, he believed. The Master's electrical power caused the sky to erupt with lightning and burned the hell out of the Wolfman, turning him into ashes. That terrified Dracula. There was no need for a silver bullet after all.

The Master's head finally lowered, and his eyes grew darker and darker. The redness burned as the evil was now full, and nothing was going to stop him.

The Master jumped through the drawbridge of the castle and walked toward the entrance. The vampires that floated in the air flew at him, taking cheap shot after cheap shot. The Master had six of them to contend with.

Dracula, meanwhile, had been hiding from The Master. It made him look weak and cowardly more than anything else, but it was for the sake of self-preservation. With great force, one of the vampires stabbed The Master with his own sword, and The Master dropped and fell to the floor. As he lay there, the vampires flew around the room, looking at him. The Master stood up and began to laugh an evil laugh that put fear into most, just as Dracula had done to generations past.

The vampires all attacked him, throwing everything they had at him, getting angrier and angrier that they could not move him. As one came near him and flew high enough above him, he pulled out his sword and launched it with great might. Throwing the sword at her, he nailed her right in the head, dropping her to the floor, stunned, and then dead.

The Master held two spears, one in each hand. A wind created in the first room of the castle carried the spears to two of the other vampires, and they couldn't shake them. The spears eventually killed them, and they crashed to the floor. The Master burned the fourth vampire with his eyes, and the other two were killed in two different ways. The Master picked up a piece of wood that had come loose from the door, and as one flew toward him, he nailed the vampire girl right in the head. As the last vampire girl came at him with a death-defying cry, he cut off her head with one swing of his sword. The bluish-skinned bodies littered the floor.

The Master had turned Dracula's band of minions into nothing more than a body count. He headed up the stairs to where Dracula waited. When he finally got to the top, Dracula tackled him and sent The Master over the banister and crashing down onto the hard floor. The Master rolled around, hurt.

Dracula saw his vampires dead and knew that the Wolfman must be dead as well. He took The Master by the skull and threw him across the room so that he crashed into the wall, then changed into bat form. The mutant vampire was ready for the second battle with the fierce warrior, fueled by the need for revenge after the warrior had killed so many of his protectors, most of all the Wolfman. The Master stood up as the mutant flew toward him. Using his spiked hand, The Master nailed him with a backhand that cut his face. The black mutant bat backed off.

The Master looked at him and said, "What? You're afraid of me and can't fight me in your human form?"

Dracula changed back into human form.

The Master stood and said, "I'm going to kill you."

Dracula responded, "I'd like for you to try."

They ran toward each other and leaped into the air, floating up to the third floor while punching the hell out of each other, though their punches had little effect. They finally got to the top, each going for a kick and knocking the other down.

Dracula grabbed the Master and slammed him up against the wall, shattering the glass from one of the paintings hanging there. Dracula followed up with a kick, which sent him airborne through a room of coffins. The Master threw a coffin at Dracula, hitting him in the head and knocking him down. The Master pushed the broken wood away from him. As The Master and Dracula got up, they both seemed unstoppable. They walked toward each other, and Dracula threw a punch, but his cape got in his way. The Master pulled it over Dracula's head, wrapped it around his neck, and repeatedly punched him in the face with his spiked hands. Each punch seemed harder than the last. Dracula could only stand a few. He dropped on one knee, then fell to the floor.

The Master kicked him in the head with his boot, and the blade that was on his boot cut his head open and caused him to bleed. The Master grabbed the back of his neck and slammed him face-first into the wood floor, leaving an imprint. The Master then ripped off Dracula's cape and saw how mangled his face was, fangs wrenched in different directions and blood pouring from the wounds on his face inflicted by the spikes.

Dracula lunged toward The Master and gave him a massive uppercut that sent him off his feet and knocked his skull sideways. Dracula got up first and went to pull The Master's leg out from under him, and got a kick to the face that caused his fangs to bleed even more. He jumped on The Master with all his force, pinned him to the floor, and tried to bite him. Instead, he broke his teeth. No one he had ever tried to bite in two hundred years had been as powerful as The Master.

Dracula was in total shock. The Master caught him off guard with a punch to the face, knocking him down to the floor on the third level. "How is that possible?" he asked.

The Master looked at him. "I can't die," he said fiercely.

Dracula scooted away from The Master, creating some distance between them. He jumped down from the third level and grabbed a spear from one of the dead vampires. The Master followed him carefully. Dracula had no idea how to deal with him. He had no defense, for the first time ever. Dracula swooped in and swung his arms and knocked The

Master off his feet, sending him into the air. He landed hard on a piece of iron.

Dracula flew up to the ceiling and grabbed the chains he had up there. As The Master began to come around, Dracula landed back on the floor, chains in hand. He ran toward The Master, and with part of a chain wrapped around his hand, used his fist to repeatedly punch him. Dracula knocked him from one side of the room to the other, beating him more fiercely with each blow.

The Master managed to stand, much to Dracula's amazement. He didn't think anyone could stand by himself after such vicious punches. Dracula then did a quick, agile flip that knocked The Master all the way back toward the entrance to where the Wolfman's secret passage was. Dracula looked around for anything that could be used as a weapon, and noticed the spear. After grabbing the rest of the chain, he picked up The Master, who appeared to have been beaten to death by the massive strikes from the chain. Dracula pulled The Master up, bound his legs and arms with the chain, and wrapped his arms tightly. He chained The Master to the bookcase so that he couldn't move. Dracula used his sharp claws and slashed at The Master's armor, only putting scratches on it and nothing more.

Dracula smiled, realizing that The Master's time was up. He went over and picked up the spear with his right hand. He looked at the carnage. Usually it was Dracula's death toll that was evident, not someone else's. The Master was bleeding, though with all the armor that covered his body, it was hard to tell how badly.

Grunting with anger, Dracula grabbed his spear and ran

toward The Master, who couldn't move. Using all the force he could muster, Dracula penetrated the armor that no one had been able to for four hundred years. A cry came from The Master that would wake any unborn animals in the Black Sea. The people of Transylvania heard something that didn't seem to fade, a cry of death. Some feared it was their last hope of surviving.

Dracula breathed heavily as he watched The Master's head fall. He noticed The Master's bloodied sword lying on the wooden floor. With a huge smile on his face, he walked over slowly and picked it up. He wiped the blood off the sword and walked toward the dead Master, whose body was still chained. Becoming angrier and angrier, he lifted up the sword and twirled it around, then cut off The Master's head.

As Dracula watched the head roll, he dropped the sword in disbelief. No blood had come out. More and more clouds filled the sky, and it got so dark that he couldn't see—dark as the depths of hell, if not darker.

All the lights went out in Transylvania. The old man and old woman knew that Dracula had tried to kill The Master. Some people ran from the village, and others stayed in their houses. The Master's head rolled and hit the leg of a coffee table. A blistering wind shattered all the windows. As Dracula looked around, even he wondered what was going on.

The skull lit up with fiery eyes and laughed as it began to float in the air. The body came alive, and The Master's arms and legs pulled on the chains, breaking first one side and then the other.

Dracula began to swing at the head. It flew around,

opened up its mouth, and set him on fire. A fierce power from the sky blew off the top of the castle, leveling it, and all that stood was the ground floor. All the peaks were destroyed. The Master's head finally went back into place. He looked at Dracula, still on fire, with a death stare.

Dracula tried to fly away. The Master beat him brutally, punching and kicking, using a variety of deadly combinations. Dracula had no answer for The Master. The kicks and the punches The Master landed caused Dracula to bleed and bleed, until he was weak at the knees.

The Master grabbed Dracula's head, tilted it back, and repeatedly beat his face until The Master's gloves were full of blood. Dracula fell to his knees. The Master gave him a kick in the back of his head, cracking his skull, and blood poured out. There was not one part of Dracula that wasn't red.

The Master held him up with his left hand and repeatedly punched him in the chest. The spikes made Dracula bleed and bleed. He was so badly beaten that nothing could have helped him. With The Master's right hand, he sent one fierce blow to the heart, putting a hole in Dracula's chest. He ripped out his heart and threw it to the ground, then ripped the upper body to shreds, as if it were a piece of paper. The Master then tore Dracula's head off and threw it to the side. He took the wooden stake the old man had given him and drove it right through Dracula's heart.

The dark sky turned red, and the red lightning slowly stopped and receded back up into the sky. The Master began to feel vibrations, and knew it was time to leave. The castle began to sink, and he grabbed his two swords and ran as fast as possible for the front door. He continued as fast as he could through the darkened graveyard and the wooded area around the castle.

The Master ran quickly. After he got through the woods, he turned and watched as the entire castle sank into the ground. As he walked back to the village, he ripped out the spear that Dracula had nailed him with.

The Master finally reached the village. Many of the villagers had come out after seeing the lightning and the dark skies that changed to red, then went back to normal. The people were all in shock after learning that he had killed Dracula. Only the old couple had thought he was capable.

The Master stood strong and tall as he walked. He didn't look hurt. He had been more than capable of winning the battle. His power certainly showed how much stronger he had been than Dracula. Most saw him as a savior, but others saw him as a monster, no different from Dracula.

The old man and old woman were the first to greet The Master. They were happy to be rid of the beast. Dracula had been such a plague on their village for so many years, and it was finally over. The other people hadn't been as confident in The Master, but he had proved he was more than capable of fulfilling his duty.

The Master was grateful, and he felt like more of a hero than he ever had in the years that he was alive. He knelt before the old man and old woman and kissed their hands. For a moment, he felt something he couldn't quite explain. He didn't exactly know what it was, but it was a great feeling. It reminded him of a feeling he had long ago when his parents were still alive. If he had been able to articulate it, he would have called it a sense of belonging.

The Master couldn't stay long. A big journey lay ahead. He had to go to Romania. He realized, though, that he had never even learned the kind old couple's names. Now he wanted to know, as they had helped him greatly. They were the closest to a family he had in that moment, though he didn't know if he'd ever see them again.

The old man grabbed his hand. "My name is Glenn, and my wife is Margaret. I am a time traveler, and so is my wife. We already know what you are going to do. But that doesn't matter right now. You need to follow the path."

The Master looked at Glenn.

"A word of advice," said Glenn as he looked into The Master's eyes. "Watch your back."

Margaret grabbed The Master's bloodied hand. "You shouldn't trust Nemesis or Albert," she added. "I see what happens to you."

"I am invincible," The Master protested. "Hasn't it been proven by now that I cannot die?"

"You might be almighty, but they will try to find a way to get rid of you. Killing you will be their focus. Not only are you more powerful than they can imagine, but you are more powerful than even *you* think you are."

"How did you become a time traveler?" The Master asked.

"That is for another conversation. But take my words to heart. You will need them. I must go and get what you will need."

"What I will need?"

"Yes, what you will need," Glenn reiterated. "I must go back to the fifteenth century."

The Master's eyes widened in surprise, and he said, "That's far back."

Glenn then slipped up and said, "Your army is waiting for you." He cringed. "Oh, damn, I shouldn't have said that." He shrugged. "Oh well, at least now you know. Yes, your army."

Glenn opened up a large portal with his hands. As a time traveler, he was able to open a portal at any time and bounce between times at will and whenever he wanted to. He was the exception among time travelers—he was the most powerful of them, and able to travel through the longest periods of time. He didn't know what it was about The Master, but for some reason, he saw something in him that others hadn't seen.

The portal opened, and Glenn and his wife went through it. It swirled in a white circle, almost as if someone were being hypnotized by its color. One minute they were there, and the next minute they were gone. It was like a dream.

The Master began to experience something that he had never felt before. Someone actually cared about him, and that was out of the ordinary. As a killing warrior, The Master wasn't one to have feelings for anyone. It was part of a long destiny that he had. Now he started to feel, for the first time in over four hundred years, that someone gave two cents about him. It brought him an odd mixture of feelings that he couldn't quite understand.

The Master was so taken by Glenn. He thought about Glenn vanishing and what Glenn had said about an army that was rising. He was confused about things he couldn't begin to understand. He only knew that Nemesis and Albert couldn't be trusted.

Now it was his turn to be advised. Finally, someone was watching out for him and guiding him to the right pathway. Glenn saw something in him that was righteous. He believed that he could be a great warrior for the right side instead of the wrong side. He could be redeemed after all of his wrongful deeds. He thought that one day, maybe, the Sword of Oman might even be in The Master's hands. Glenn was the only one who knew the hiding place of the legendary sword. Over time, no one had been able to overcome the great warrior who protected it, though many had tried, unsuccessfully.

Glenn had plans for The Master, it was true, but he also had his own mission to complete. Still, Glenn knew that one day The Master would rewrite history and get the Sword of Oman. He felt that truth resonate within him, as if it were inevitable.

Chapter 6

The Master headed toward the beautiful city of Bucharest, not knowing where Albert and Nemesis were. Wearing a brown monk's outfit that Glenn had given him, he found a ride on a bus. Glenn knew he wouldn't be welcomed warmly by the people of the beautiful European city.

As The Master finally entered the city, he saw that it wasn't all that big, though it was big enough for someone who was still trying to get used to Manhattan. He walked a few blocks, observing the little stores that looked as if they belonged in this unique area of Europe. He knew he was certainly somewhere far from home. The European setting was something he was not used to, with everything so nice and clean. The Master had no idea where to find Albert and Nemesis, or even if he *would* find them.

He bumped into a few people, knocking them to the ground with little care or acknowledgment. A couple of police officers started following the suspicious figure in the brown outfit.

The Master stopped in his tracks and looked at the cobblestone ground. "It would be wise for you not to follow me," he said, then turned and started to walk away.

One of the police officers grabbed his arm. The Master sliced his hand with his spikes, instantly soaking the hand in blood. The other officer started to call for backup, but The Master took the radio, stuck it down his throat, and killed him through suffocation. The officer who was bleeding twisted The Master's neck, trying to break it.

The Master took off his cloak. There stood the tall and dark Master, with his skull and beady red eyes. In front of the Palace of the Romanian Parliament he stood, eliciting cries and yells of fear.

Albert and Nemesis appeared out of nowhere right at that moment. The Master headed in one direction, while Nemesis went toward the back of the building and through the heavily guarded parking lot. There were two main ways to get in and out of the building. Since Nemesis was a military robot, he could jam all the doors so that no one could leave, and that he did.

The Master noticed dark clouds overhead, and the sky became as dark as night. He walked past the large water fountain that was not far from the huge parking lot; the lot looked as big as an NFL football field. It had large black gates and a stone road that led all around the building. As The Master approached, security forces swarmed the parking lot. Something was afoot.

Inside, they were trying to get security up in the building and really thought they had a fault in the system. President

Vladimir Vooden was present in Parliament for the first time since his vacation.

Security and police officers surrounded the building. When they saw Nemesis on the south side and heard gunshots, many realized the gravity of the situation. They rushed for the door, but it was locked. The Master approached the black gates to the parking lot. With one punch, he shattered the gates, which were electrically wired, which in turn shattered the entire parking lot. Most men were scared, as they should be, by the man with the gleaming skull. He had his two swords in his hands and didn't look as if he were listening to anyone, staring intently ahead, on a purposeful path.

A man got on a microphone and told his soldiers to get ready to open fire on The Master. The Master wasn't stopping, and most of the soldiers were all too anxious to obey the command. They were scared, and every man feared the worst. The collective thought on that cold, wintry day in Romania was: *How could this happen and why?*

The Master had nothing on but his armor. It was as if he felt nothing and feared nothing, either.

The soldiers received the call to open fire, and they readily fired and kept on unloading round after round, until the smoke got so thick that they couldn't see. After the smoke, rain, and fog began to settle in from the storm, the dust settled, only for an evil laugh to emerge and echo across the sky.

"You fools," a voice said. "You can't kill The Master. Haven't you learned?"

They all had terrified looks on their faces. Everyone

knew who this was, thanks to Twitter and Facebook. (News traveled fast now with social media.) Twenty or thirty men all ran around the cars in the parking lot. The Master lifted his hands up in the air, and one by one, all the cars were catapulted and exploded, as if mini bombs had gone off. Some soldiers had been sitting in them, trying to get a good shot through the windows. Instead, they wound up dead.

As The Master moved his left and right hands from one side of his body to the other, the movement removed the fog from the parking lot. The men realized that no mere guns were going to stop The Master. The men of Parliament watched, hoping and praying that this man would die.

No one had any communication because Nemesis had jammed everything. Even cell phones wouldn't work. With his two swords, The Master did what he knew best how to do—he killed. All the bullets that they shot at him bounced off his body, not even denting or scratching any part of him. The blood from each swipe of his swords grew darker and darker with each kill. The Master never let go of his swords, no matter how he was outnumbered, and he fought and killed all the guards. The white snow was turned red. A massacre had begun.

It had made the front page that he had killed Dracula, but these men never looked at the front page unless it involved politics. As The Master had what seemed like the entire army in front of the Parliament, Nemesis began to walk. His feet shook the ground, and everyone realized something unprecedented and enormous was coming. They were going to be surrounded by two vicious enemies—one of whom wouldn't die. When they turned around to see the pharaoh-like robot of Nemesis, they knew they were doomed.

The soldiers began to fire their AK-47s at the Master with no effect, the only recourse they had left. But he simply cleaned off his swords with the snow, and then stood up and charged the soldiers from one end and then the other.

Guns came out from Nemesis's arms, and he began to shoot at everything. With every type of gun at his disposal, he was impossible to stop. The more soldiers who came, the more he killed. They all died trying to stop the vicious foe, and their sacrifice was for nothing.

As Nemesis and The Master killed off the rest of the soldiers, they turned around and saw the tanks the Romanian military had sent. The tanks coming toward the Parliament building destroyed the large fountains. Two people had taken so many lives and caused the high body count in the parking lot, and the military was getting more scared by the second, since their president was in that building, and they were sworn to protect him above all else.

The Master, Albert, and Nemesis were intent on trying to locate the cold fusion formula and activate the time machine. But they hadn't any idea where to begin to look for the formula. What they did know how to do was kill, and they were very good at that—a great talent, at least for a consortium of villains.

The Master stood and watched Nemesis, thinking of what Glenn had told him. He began to notice how quick the robot was, and how he was made of solid metal. The Master knew that if Nemesis ever turned, it would be quite difficult to stop something that strong. He watched from a distance as Nemesis headed into the bloodied snow. He watched as he shot at everyone, killing them easily and dropping them like flies. It was as if he feared nothing. But The Master began to see things that Albert probably wouldn't have noticed right away. It was as if Nemesis was starting to take over his own computer system. *How is that possible?* The Master didn't think it was, but he didn't know for certain. The Master knew he had to watch his back, and that was what he intended to do.

As Nemesis stood in front of the tanks and all the dead bodies that surrounded him, a tank fired at him, missing him, but hitting the Master instead, sending him reeling from the explosion, his head blown back. Nemesis opened his hands, and from all ten fingers came mini missiles that hit both tanks, causing massive explosions that sent the tanks sky high. There were some assorted soldiers who remained scattered, and some of them saw The Master's head flying around, but they didn't believe what they were seeing. The Master's head—how was that possible?

"He's dead," one soldier said.

"It's impossible," said another. "You can't kill him."

The soldiers ran, and Nemesis turned his head. Albert watched from a distance and began to realize the power of The Master. The Master's disembodied head flew after the soldiers as they all ran and hid in the marketplace. His eyes were all black now—not the red eyes that many had seen. The sight was terrifying.

As he flew and looked to see if anyone could be found, a dark beam came out of The Master's eyes, covering the entire area. His eyes skinned the bodies of the soldiers from head to toe, and then took their souls. Blood came pouring out of soldiers, from wherever they were in their different hiding spots. Pools of blood formed every which way in the area.

The more Albert saw, the more he began to fear The Master. It was scary to be connected with him. How could he trust something no one could kill? It was impossible. The Master was more powerful than Albert had ever thought he was, almost like a god. Albert knew that he had to somehow get rid of him, and that it would not be easy. There would only be one way, he resolved—to send him back in time through the time machine. Albert had the perfect plan for when they got back to New York, but he needed that formula in order to do it. That was where the president came in. Albert knew he had to get the cold fusion formula, or the consequences could be dire.

As The Master's head floated back onto his body and reattached itself, Nemesis looked on, amazed. He had never seen anything like it. Albert and Nemesis both felt that The Master could kill them. Meanwhile, Nemesis was beginning to take over the program that ran him and was becoming more like a human, which seemed strange. But they now all had one common, clear goal—obtaining the formula that was hidden somewhere in the Parliament building. They had to find out where, and they would stop at nothing in order to do so.

The men of Romania were terrified. Soldiers were lying dead all over. It was a war, but the army hadn't won. How could this have happened? The Master was a deadly warrior, and Nemesis was controlled for the most part by Albert. He, too, was changing, but the worst was yet to come. His look and his intentions grew more and more evil. He had a smile of pure destruction and death spread over his face, as if he knew that things were going to become deadlier than ever. If and when he ever got hold of the energy source, it was going to be the end of The Master.

Albert knew The Master was stronger than he had ever thought. He had killed Dracula and lived, and then had been blown up by a tank and still survived. The Master had proven he was something extraordinary.

But at times The Master still didn't really know who he was. Glenn had shown him that he had a softer, more humane side, a side he never knew he had. If there was a way he could go back and see things in another light, would things be different in his life? What was the purpose of all the training he went through? Glenn saw The Master as something that most didn't—he saw him as human. No one had ever seen him that way. Everyone saw him as a monster capable of destruction. With a gleaming skull for a head, how could they see him as anything else?

As Albert watched The Master, he thought he seemed hesitant at times to do things. The Master appeared to have a human side, and Albert began to see the skulled warrior as a monster he could control. Nemesis would indeed come in quite handy.

With the soldiers outside left for dead, Nemesis unlocked the doors to the Palace of the Romanian Parliament and was the first to walk into the huge building. Albert, who had been there many years before, had a map of the building's layout and was able to direct him. Its size made the White House look like a miniature. Nemesis, with the physique of a pharaoh made of chrome and high-tech equipment, looked very intimidating. How could anything challenge him? The world would be in for many changes if Nemesis got rid of The Master. The world needed a hero. The comics always created someone to look up to, but that was all just a fantasy.

Albert had a perfect sense of direction in the large structure and sent Nemesis straight for the Parliament room. The Master stood in back of them, feeling like a pawn or a third party. He was still getting used to a world that had no feeling to it. In a way, he missed his old one, that of constant fighting. He had often wondered how the world would be if those things had never happened. Glenn had told him that, soon enough, a war was coming—something about the rise of dark lords. He often thought about that. He didn't yet understand what Glenn meant, but he knew that in time, he would. Glenn was a true friend, he realized. He was looking out for him, something The Master wasn't used to.

Albert had Nemesis break down the door so they could go in and find the president of Romania. Albert carried a gun in his hand and walked behind Nemesis. He warned the Parliament that if they tried to stop him, everyone in the room would die.

All the men backed off.

"Where is the president?" Albert asked.

No one on either side of the room answered, though there was a lot of mumbling. Just like politicians to be noncommital about something. When The Master walked in as if ready to kill, they all got a glimpse of the terrifying warrior. Carrying the two swords on his back, he herded everyone to one side of the room. The Master knew they were hiding the president. He felt his presence. With his deep and menacing voice, he stated that if the president didn't come out, they all would die. The Master violently began to move their desks as easily as if he were ripping paper. He angrily flung them all over the room.

The Master grabbed the nearest man and lifted him up with one hand. "Where is he?" The Master demanded.

The man looked down and pointed to a small trapdoor in the floor. The Master dropped the man, ripped up the trapdoor, and found the president of the country, shaking. He was as scared as a mouse cornered by a cat. The politicians were protecting him from death.

The Master grabbed him and threw him to the floor. He drew his sword up to the man's throat. "Where is the cold fusion formula?"

President Vooden moved very carefully. With The Master's sword at his neck, he didn't want to make any sudden moves.

Albert looked at the president. "Where is it?" he asked with a loud voice. "Give it to me."

The Master grabbed Vooden with great force and got an answer very quickly. The sixty-five-year-old president had never thought that the formula would bring him this much trouble. One formula to create good now had the possibility of being used for evil. How had this come to be?

The Master followed him with his sword in one hand and kept a constant watch as he walked on the red carpet, passing by busts of former great leaders and paintings on the wall that seemed like something out of a museum or magazine. Large chandeliers hung from the ceiling. The Master followed him down hallways and around corners and up the stairs through door after door. The Master was getting impatient with the long walk.

Vooden finally came to a door and took out his keys. He opened the door and went to the painting on the wall that looked like the painting of Adam and Eve at the American Museum of Natural History in New York. He moved the painting and opened the safe, then took out the piece of paper containing the formula. With shaking hands, he gave it to The Master.

The Master handed it to Albert, who was behind Nemesis. The Master looked at the president and granted his freedom, taking the sword away from this throat. Albert looked at the Master and hit him in his skull.

The Master grabbed Albert and threw him into the chair situated at the president's desk, breaking the chair. The Master stood over him. "Is today a good day to die?" he asked. "I don't have time for people being foolish. If you want to die, I will grant your wish."

"I'm sorry," Albert said. "Do you have the formula?"

The Master looked behind him. Nemesis had drawn his guns as if trying to save his father from a brutal death. A feeling overtook The Master, like one he remembered from long ago. He handed the formula to Albert but held on to it with a strong grip.

"Know this," he said to Albert. "If you ever dare to hit me or double-cross me, I will kill you and your robot. You can't kill *me*, but I will make sushi of *you*—and of Nemesis, I will make scrap."

The Master let go, and Albert finally had the formula. As they all left the building and headed back to the dock, Albert knew The Master was becoming more of a problem and that it was time to get rid of him. They had some traveling to do, but maybe the best way to get rid of The Master was to dump him in the Black Sea. It was said that all types of demons and dark animals guarded it, and that no one entered, and no one left.

Nemesis had gotten a new boat, different from the one they came on. The Master seemed angry. He knew something was entirely wrong. Glenn had told him to be careful of his surroundings. Albert got on the boat and left, attempting to get as far away as possible. The Master saw the little rowboat disappear in the fog and mist of the night. Nemesis knew what had to be done. The Master was now being ignited in a dangerous way.

Nemesis looked straight into the eyes of The Master, and The Master returned the stare. Many people around saw this happening and ran in pure fear. No one wanted to be around when the two did battle.

"You are going to die," Nemesis said.

The Master smiled. Anything related to fighting was music to his ears. Nemesis grabbed The Master and threw him so high that he landed on a farm miles away. As The Master came crashing down on a barn, the barn collapsed, and all the farm animals came running out.

Nemesis flew over to where the Master had landed and floated over the barn. The Master brushed himself off, grabbed a piece of wood from the rubble that remained of the barn, and waited for Nemesis. The Master was being smart, hiding from Nemesis. He now was the hunted.

Nemesis came crashing through an already broken

barn, sending even more splintered siding and wood in all directions. As Nemesis landed, The Master jumped up, swinging a large piece of wood and sending Nemesis through the only remaining upright wall of the barn, making it collapse on The Master. Nemesis landed not too far away in a cornfield, though nothing was growing now in the wintry cold of Romania.

As The Master stood up, the large pile of wood and hay began to move. Most people would not have gotten up, but The Master did. He walked with a purpose: he wanted Nemesis dead. He had his two swords in his hands, and all his spikes on his hands and feet were ready to inflict some serious damage. The Master was now out in the wintry cold of Romania. But how could a man like The Master survive the dark and cold? Was the human part of him enough to cause him weakness when faced with a natural force?

Nemesis came flying up from the cornfield, grabbed The Master, and flew him straight down into the ground, leaving behind a large hole. Then he picked him up and threw him into a large tree with such force that he cracked the trunk. The Master fell down and held his back as if hurt. As The Master lay on the ground and writhed, Nemesis walked over to him. The Master still had his swords, but his body hid them. Subtly, he tightened his fingers around the swords, readying himself.

Nemesis grabbed The Master with both hands. The Master opened his eyes and swung his sword, cutting off half of Nemesis's face. The pharaoh-like robot dropped The Master. The Master grabbed him and repeatedly punched him in the face and the body, leaving dents with his spiked fists. Nemesis's electrical work was badly damaged, and sparks flew from the robot every so often. Nemesis shot at The Master with all his might, but the guns had no effect.

The Master began to use his mighty hands and feet on Nemesis. He had him right where he wanted him. Nemesis was about to become a pile of scrap. He started crawling away, as if looking for someone to help him, but no one was going to help him—no one was anywhere in sight.

As Nemesis got up, The Master punched him with his spiked hand. The Master removed his right arm from its place. Nemesis turned around and punched The Master in the face with his left arm, hurtling him away from the damaged robot. One more hit would deal a severe blow to Albert's end game. The Master was certainly putting a wrench in the carefully laid plans.

Nemesis was growing weak and losing fluid. His circuits were damaged, and The Master was winning a fight that Albert never thought would be possible for him to win. Nemesis opened his one hand, and out came mini bombs that latched on to The Master's body, not making a single scratch on it. From the explosions, it looked as if The Master's body would be in several pieces. It was not. He lay on the ground, as if he were merely unconscious.

As Nemesis took his time staggering to an upright position, The Master's swords were nowhere to be seen. Nemesis was finally on his feet, a destroyed robot missing half a face and an arm. He was the worse of the two foes. Nemesis got up and grabbed his cut-off face and his robot arm. He flew with The Master holding on to him with one arm. They both landed near the docks. The Master repeatedly punched him. It didn't seem to have much effect, even with the damaged chest of his. Nemesis was running on little power. He never thought that The Master would be able to take him on. A majority of his systems were shut down, but Nemesis had a few things left to dish out to The Master. He resolved that it was time to finish The Master off once and for all, no matter the cost.

The Master and Nemesis were by the water, and Albert, who watched from the nearby boat, was in total disbelief that Nemesis, a superior military robot, was so badly damaged. To most it wouldn't be too surprising, since The Master was superior to everyone else.

Nemesis kicked The Master in the ribs and sent him through the window of a building, breaking the window frame with the impact. As Nemesis walked, sparks flew everywhere. Some of the loose material that was flammable caught fire. Nemesis walked through the fire and out for the kill. He picked up an ax, and as The Master came running toward Nemesis, Nemesis threw the ax, hitting The Master in the shoulder. The Master started to bleed. He dropped the sword that he had in his hands and fell to the ground.

As Albert watched in disbelief, Nemesis leaned on a pole as if he were about to explode. The brightness of the fire lit up the sky and exposed the damage from the battle. It was unfathomable what would have happened to Albert if The Master had won. Nemesis was as powerful if not stronger than The Master was when it came to technology. Nemesis saw The Master lying on the ground and knew it was his time to get rid of him, for good.

Nemesis had been leaning on the pole. Now he ripped

it off the dock with his one hand. It came crashing down on The Master, and the torn electrical wires caused more explosions. Nemesis grabbed the wires, ripped them off the pole, and wrapped them around The Master's neck. Choking, The Master coughed and gasped for air. He used his free hand to punch Nemesis in the face and loosen the tight grip that Nemesis had on his neck. As The Master lay on the ground, gasping for air, Nemesis ran as fast as he could. The Master finally caught his breath. He got to his feet and followed Nemesis.

Nemesis spotted a large yacht near the part of the dock that wasn't burning. He ran toward it and jumped on it. The Master wasn't that far behind him, though Nemesis had a good head start. The Master was the more powerful of the two, based on pure strength. No one was as powerful as The Master. When it came to machinery, though, Nemesis had the advantage. He was far superior to anything that was out there.

The Master was pure evil, but he had his hands full with Nemesis. Only The Master was capable of taking him down and destroying him. As The Master finally caught up, he jumped on the yacht with Nemesis. They stood toe-to-toe, The Master with sweat dripping down his skull—the skull that so many had come to fear. So many victims had that skull as their last image before they died at his hand. The fire seemed to burn and burn, creating a heavy smoke that blocked their vision.

From the boat, Albert saw how destroyed Nemesis was. Albert knew he needed to get out of Romania, and with Nemesis in one piece. He needed him to complete his plan.

He couldn't complete it without him. Albert had the guns from the Navy vessel that had gotten them there tucked away in a bag in the boat, along with a rocket launcher. He got in the water and pulled the boat as close to the fire as possible without getting burned. To get a clear shot of the skull-man was impossible. The Master delivered punch after punch, and the robot was getting destroyed worse and worse with each passing second. The pharaoh-like Nemesis had all of his wires showing, and a face that was half ripped apart. He was a complete mess.

As The Master punched and kicked, the spikes on his hands did a great deal of damage, and it was hard to imagine that Nemesis was going to win the fight. He began to sink farther and farther toward the bottom of the boat, and The Master's brutal force of power made Nemesis clearly look like the weaker opponent. The robot began to spark. The Master picked the robot up, lifted him above his head, and launched him into the Black Sea.

Albert, who wasn't too far from where he landed, couldn't believe his eyes. He loaded the rocket launcher and launched the rocket, causing a huge explosion and destroying the yacht and the dock, along with everything nearby. The explosions created deafening noises, and fire from the explosions filled the air and turned it red. Albert threw the rocket launcher down and swam over to where Nemesis floated. With a great effort, he got him into the boat. He was on his own to try to get back to New York.

Albert didn't stick around to see if The Master was dead or alive. How could anyone survive an explosion like that? It seemed impossible. But Albert didn't know that The Master was immortal and no ordinary being. He wasn't dead, but lay floating in the Black Sea, motionless. He was eventually pulled underwater by things that were not known or seen.

All Albert knew was that The Master was nowhere to be seen, and Nemesis was halfway destroyed. Albert wouldn't be able to make any significant repairs until he got back to New York, where his shop was. He would have to make those repairs.

Albert was now on his long journey back to New York, but not with The Master after all. Having the Master gone would make things a great deal easier, but Nemesis gone or needing serious repairs would make them much more challenging.

Chapter 7

Takeo and Matt went from a very cold environment in Japan to a very hot, humid one in the Amazon. They exchanged their winter jackets for shorts and short sleeves. They knew the Amazon to be a dangerous place, with its vast array of reptiles, insects, and other animals. They also knew that the Amazon contains two-thirds of the world's plants, the Amazon River is the largest in South America, and the Arapaima is the largest fish in the world, sometimes weighing up to four hundred pounds. There are over forty thousand plant species, over three thousand fresh-water species, and three hundred different reptiles. There are around thirty million people who rely on the resources of the mighty river. There are also 350 different ethnic groups who make up the population of the Amazon.

Matt and Takeo arrived in a village where no one spoke any English. Matt felt at home in an area where other languages were spoken, as if he were going through Chinatown in New

York City. Takeo, on the other hand, wasn't able to help. Other than English, he only knew Japanese.

The two approached the small village with its many huts. Judging by their appearance, the people had become a product of their environment. Matt and Takeo carried swords and guns and knew what they had to find. They had to find the *hobbs* plant near the sacred temple that was deep in the Amazon forest.

Matt and Takeo knew that their journey had just begun. Convincing someone to get them to the temple would certainly be a challenge. As they walked through the dirt-filled village, they pondered how they had no idea how to initiate a conversation with the villagers. They did observe how, being not too far from the Amazon River, the people found it easy to grow crops. A well line that ran directly into the village served as their main water source.

Matt and Takeo had arrived at an opportune time. They walked around and explored but stayed in the area of the village, looking at the different things that the village people were working on. A large ethnic group in this particular location was the most dangerous of them all. It was closest to the Amazon temple. With the roars and screams that came from the forest, the people never knew what predator might attack them or possibly eat them.

Tigerman was a prime specimen of a warrior, half tiger and half beast. He was one of the few that guarded the forest and the entrance to the temple. Tigerman carried a bow and arrow and had poisonous arrows that would kill within twenty-four hours, after leaving their target immobilized.

Giant Man was a giant who looked like a knight. He was

ten feet tall, with armor from head to toe, and carried a large ax capable of doing serious damage.

Gargoyles watched over the temple and dived down on anyone who came too close. They would drag them away with their mighty claws—that is, if they didn't drop them in the Amazon River for the crocodiles to feast on.

Then there was Goron, a mighty gorilla with six arms, who possessed double the strength and twice the height of a regular gorilla. His bite could instantly decapitate his prey.

Matt and Takeo thought it was going to be impossible to get past these mighty monsters.

Matt found a large building that had concrete walls. He got Takeo, and the village people ran as if they knew something was wrong. Takeo and Matt had a feeling that it could be bad. Takeo saw a sign that said: *Do not disturb the mighty Gore and Zoron.* He drew his swords and opened the door, then entered the area of the large building where Zoron and the mighty Gore rested. A huge roar greeted him as they both awoke.

Takeo and Matt took off into a run. Zoron pulled back on the mighty Gore, a large animal, as he, too, was large. Zoron was a powerful warrior, but not a human one. He was a hobgoblin: half human and half beast, with mighty fangs and a shield that held spikes on it. His armor covered his chest and legs, and his sword was a curved one that was greater than any Matt and Takeo had seen before. He wore a metal helmet over his head that left the eyes exposed and able to see. He wore armguards, his boots came up to his knees, and he had a belt that held other weapons for close battles.

Zoron held the mighty Gore to keep him from running

after them. The mighty Gore's mouth dripped with blood as if it had freshly fed on someone or something. Matt and Takeo didn't want to become the beast's next snack. Gore had quieted down, so Zoron walked over and looked down upon the two men.

"So, this is who the last wizard sent," he said. Zoron turned his back and started to walk away.

"Wait," Takeo commanded, straightening his posture and steadying his voice.

"For what? Puny humans, I was awakened because of you. I protect and fight for my people and destroy any threat that might cause them harm. I don't need to help you."

A small dwarf, with a long white beard and pure white clothes that covered him from head to toe, handed him a magic orb. Zoron gave him a nasty look. The magic dwarf, frightened, ran and hid behind Matt. Zoron took the orb into his hand and opened it. A big bright flash blinded everyone. It was a magic orb given to the dwarf by the wizard to try to help Zoron. He watched as it depicted how The Master had destroyed New York.

It had no meaning for Zoron until he saw the wizard. "The wizard of time is dying," he said, filled with rage. "He's been poisoned. Who did this? I want to kill him." He turned to Matt and Takeo. "All right, I will help you. What do you need?"

"We need to get to the Amazon temple," Matt said, relieved at Zoron's acquiescence.

"You are out of your mind," Zoron said. "What do you need in the temple?"

Takeo replied, "The hobbs plant."

Matt added, "By the time the days are up, all the evil will rise from the dead."

"Yes, I know," Zoron said. "I witnessed that many centuries ago, and furthermore, I was one of the ones who stopped it the first time. That is why my resting place is here. I am still alive for my heroic effort to save the world. Every time has its own particular fights."

Just then, the magic dwarf came out from hiding and was jumping up and down as if he had to pee. The dwarf put his hands together, and an image appeared. The dwarf also had some magic powers and was able to see things. Zoron, Matt, and Takeo all watched, and they saw Nemesis with Albert, en route to New York from Romania. The Master wasn't with them.

Matt and Takeo looked at each other. "What the hell is going on?" Matt asked.

They were at a loss. A lot had been happening that they didn't know about.

Matt looked at the small magic dwarf. "Tell me, is The Master dead?"

Takeo and Matt waited for a response. It was hard to believe someone who had destroyed an entire city could change, but they had begun to realize that The Master had started to change—somewhat.

The magic dwarf took them all into his hut and showed them some things that he could, without telling them things that they could not know.

"Yes, he is still alive," the dwarf finally answered, "and you will need everything that he has to defeat your enemy.

You will have to save him in order to win the fight. Without him, you can't win the war."

Zoron said, "It is getting late. It is time to go to sleep. I will call upon my army in the morning. Keep your weapons close."

"Why?" Matt asked.

"It has been a while since an attack," Zoron said.

Matt and Takeo looked at each other, and both had a shared feeling of dread. They weren't prepared for this at all.

Takeo tried to crack a joke. "At least Sherry doesn't know anything about what's going on."

"Oh my God, I've been gone for weeks," Matt said.

"Well, it will be a very long time before we get back," Takeo said. "She'll have to live with it, man. You were away for over ten years. A couple of weeks won't hurt at all."

Matt smiled. "I guess you're right."

Matt and Takeo sat by the fire, eating what the village people had made. Matt and Takeo didn't ask, nor did they want to know what they were eating. Most of the villagers were dark-skinned, like Indians, with the men wearing nearly nothing—a very old way of living. The women covered themselves, for the most part. The men, it was plain to see, were good warriors.

Their new ally Zoron sat on the ground and looked up at the sky with his rugged and dark countenance. He mumbled something, but neither Matt nor Takeo could understand it. As the fire burned on, the villagers gradually headed into their little huts for the night one by one. It was hard to understand this whole new world and the death threats that they were facing. The stars in the sky seemed to dim their light. If that meant something, Matt and Takeo had no clue what.

Zoron and the mighty Gore went to their own resting place. Gore rested just as any beast would, lying down in the calm before the storm. Zoron never explained what his mumbled, cryptic words were, nor did Matt or Takeo ask. They felt as if something bad was going to happen.

Nightfall had come, and the roars and howling from the mysterious beings were permeating the air. It was a terrifying feeling, and to hear them on a daily basis or even live through them was unimaginable. Zoron slept in what seemed like a palace, but why did he never protect his people? Before they went to sleep—or attempted to—the dwarf told Matt and Takeo that the creatures wouldn't try to kill Zoron because he was much too powerful. Not even the greatest creatures would dare find or kill him. He rested in the village. Only when he crossed the line between the village and the forest would the creatures attack him.

Matt knew that there was more to the story. "How the hell is Zoron alive?" he probed.

The dwarf answered, "He is alive and doesn't age because of the honor he swore to the sixth wizard. He is their warrior on Earth and sleeps here because here is the only place the realm can open in South America."

"I guess that makes sense, somewhat," Matt said. He had more questions than answers and was trying to get to the truth. Takeo, meanwhile, wasn't one for questions, but he always wanted to get results.

Matt saw the dwarf stretch out his arms as far as his small frame would allow. Matt stayed up, as the dwarf and

Takeo both headed to their rightful places to rest. Takeo's bed wasn't a comfortable bed, but it was something that would have to suffice under the circumstances. A lot of things were mysterious, and Matt found it hard to believe that The Master had turned on Nemesis. This was puzzling and made him curious. It was as if things were going the way that they weren't supposed to. *But then again,* Matt thought, *people control their own fate.*

Darkness covered the sky, and it seemed as if something or *someone* was coming. The rumblings, the vibration from the ground—what was going on? Zoron was awakened, along with Matt and Takeo. Something had disturbed the Core, though for now, Matt and Takeo had no idea what the Core was. There were two places it was kept, and only three people could disrupt the Core.

Zoron explained to Matt and Takeo how The Core was kept near the end of the Amazon River. The other Core was kept at the bottom of the Black Sea. It was a powerful weapon that could bring darkness to Earth, and there was only so much time to shut it down.

"How do you shut it down?" Matt asked.

Zoron responded, "I don't know. I wasn't around when it happened the first time. I believe we have time."

The dwarf came out, limping with his gimpy leg, having heard the conversation. He spoke to the group. "The Core has never been destroyed. There is no one who can destroy it. You would almost have to be immortal to destroy it."

Matt looked at the dwarf and asked, "No human can destroy it?"

"If you are thinking about letting The Master destroy it, good luck," Zoron said.

"We need to get to the temple, and we need to do that first," said Matt.

Zoron said, "We'll start our journey to get the hobbs plant. You'll need that in order to save the eighth wizard—if he is even still alive."

Zoron asked for help from some of the village people who understood the circumstances and what this was coming to. A war was fast approaching, and Zoron knew they needed as much help as they could possibly get. The Amazon rainforest was very big, and deadly animals, along with unfathomable things they couldn't begin to understand awaited as threats.

Matt knew things weren't right, but it was a journey that had to be faced. Now it wasn't only the safety of Sherry he was concerned about. This was something far bigger than anything that they could have possibly anticipated, with far-reaching consequences.

Matt followed Zoron as he rode the mighty Gore. The others were on foot. Some men stayed behind to protect the village in case anything came to attack the people left in the village. The Core was broken, and now that it was, anything was allowed entry.

The sky became dark around the entire world for just a few seconds, from New York to Germany to Japan to India. A voice in the sky said, "Aramids is coming. I am alive, and I am coming." An evil laugh filled the air, and the face of the man that was Aramids appeared. Then the image disappeared, and the sky went back to the way it was.

Takeo grinned, which let on to the others that he knew who Aramids was.

Matt looked at him. "Who the hell is he?" he asked Takeo.

Takeo answered, "A man you don't want to know. Let's get to the temple."

The Amazon was hot and buggy, extremely humid, and very dangerous. A lot of poisonous snakes, insects, and other lethal animals and monsters awaited them. It was treacherous as they traveled down through the shrubs and other plants, not always being able to see what was on the ground. In the vast area that split through the forest, they went down the riverbank, watching for any crocodiles hiding in green areas. That they had to be careful was an understatement. On the way, they did lose a few men to crocs, as was normal. The crocs took them into the water and made short work of them.

Zoron couldn't worry about a few mere men. He had other concerns. His mission was to try to get Matt and Takeo what they needed. The hobbs plant was the one plant that had the power to cure anything. How could that one plant do that? Matt decided not to ask questions anymore, since he was learning very quickly through the experiences. The Amazon was vast, and it had its difficult ways about it. The trees were tall, and the rainforest talked. What it said depended on its mood, and you never knew what that would be. Zoron knew that at some point they were going to be attacked.

Matt's and Takeo's eyes searched all around. It was a very eerie and unsettling place, and it was only dusk. "I wouldn't want to be here at night," Matt said quietly to himself. He had his reservations about being there, but no matter how he felt, he was determined to complete what had to be done. Matt and Takeo didn't have much time to get back to Japan with the cure for the wizards.

As Zoron rode the mighty Gore, he used a sword to cut any of the tree branches that were in his way. Matt and Takeo itched constantly from the bites of mosquitos and dragonflies that flew in their faces. There were many sounds in the forest, and Takeo looked all over, but it was hard to discern where everything was coming from. The villagers stayed behind and held their arrows closely, ready to let them go at any turn.

Zoron heard the rumblings of something. The noise grew louder and louder, and he sensed that something big was near. He warned Matt, and the villagers climbed up the trees to get ready for whatever might be coming. They all knew the forest. Matt and Takeo did not, but they were learning. The rumblings got bigger and bigger, but Zoron and Gore weren't small, either. They were both very large creatures. Matt and Takeo watched as whatever it was got closer and closer, and bushes and trees were pushed and knocked down violently.

Then it revealed itself. What had come at them was a giant green ogre. He had massive biceps and triceps, wore ripped pants that looked as black as coal, and held a sharp and deadly sword. He had battle guards that went up to his elbows on both of his arms. His chest was bare, and he wore some type of worship chain around his neck.

Zoron got off of Gore and raced toward the giant ogre. The large half bear–half panther lunged with one great leaping motion. An animal of that size could knock over anyone, no matter how big he was. The ogre had his battle club. Both of them jumped in midair and had the same agenda in mind.

The villagers started firing their arrows at the ogre, only taking clear shots to make sure that they didn't hit the mighty Gore, whose jaws dripped with blood and saliva. The powerful Gore snapped his neck, trying to bite the ogre's head off with his large teeth. He was having problems containing the ogre, as the beast's body was so large and powerful. The two mammoth creatures rolled around, crashing into trees and breaking them, and crushing anything that lay in their paths.

The ogre finally had a good grip and launched Gore into the air, breaking more trees in the process. The ogre got up and got a huge fist from Zoron, right to the side of the head, a bone-crushing shot that knocked his helmet cleanly off his head. The ogre landed on the ground.

Zoron stood right on top of him, so the ogre was unable to use his strength. Zoron picked him up by the horns and lifted him way over his head, giving him a mighty suplex, causing them both to land on their backs. One of the ogre's horns had broken off, and green blood gushed from the affected area. Zoron, the first to get up, took the horn in his hand. Then the ogre got up slowly, his face covered with his oozing blood. The mighty Gore was hiding in the bushes and jumped on the ogre's back, biting and clawing his back and head ferociously. The villagers stayed in the treetops, hoping none of the trees would come down. It would be a mighty fall if they did.

The ogre yelled in pain as the mighty Gore hacked at

him. The ogre fell to the ground, biting and using its claws that were sharp as nails. He was one beast not to mess with, but now his life was over, as the mighty Gore tore him apart.

His big pile of guts and blood left a lingering odor that added just one more scent to permeate the forest, a reminder of the battle that had just taken place.

"Watch out," Zoron said. "He was one of the four monsters that guard the Amazon temple."

Zoron knew they were getting close. They had spent hours going down the path that he had found many centuries ago. It wasn't an easy path to take, but it saved time, and Zoron knew that time was not on their side. Eliminating the giant ogre was one step, but it would get increasingly difficult as they grew closer to the temple.

Matt and Takeo were shocked at the things the forest held. Takeo had some understanding of what was happening, and he knew the time was coming when they both would need to help Zoron and the mighty Gore.

"Who are the other three that guard the Amazon temple?" Matt asked.

"Well," Zoron answered, "the Giant Man was the last of them, also the hardest to defeat. He was the strongest of them all. Then, the gargoyles stay on top of the temple and watch for anything that comes near. They are strong, always watching from above. But the dangerous ones are yet to come."

Zoron asked the small dwarf for the magic orb. "I am going to need help." Even though Zoron was not a creature from hell, he had some magical qualities, but only for the use of good.

The dwarf grunted. He was hesitant to give it to Zoron.

"If you don't give it to me, I will make sure you are the first one eaten," Zoron told him.

The dwarf handed the orb over to Zoron, who took it in his large hands with their long nails. The dwarf said some magical words, and with that, Zoron was granted the help of the Kobbads.

The Kobbads were lizard warriors, with razor-sharp nails and teeth. They were fast and agile, carried bows and arrows on their backs, and had good sight for shooting. On their waists they carried small swords. They weren't big, but they wore some protective armor. Most of their skin was dark brown, which blended in with the trees.

Matt followed Zoron, the villagers followed them, and Takeo brought up the rear. Matt carried his sword and guns, but he had a feeling these things wouldn't be enough. Zoron and the men from the village saw something moving closer and closer. It was a skeleton warrior. Matt drew his sword, and Takeo had a sword in each hand. Others had their small swords in their hands. The lizard warriors went up the trees and shot their arrows.

Matt innately sensed that something huge was coming.

"We must find our way to the temple," Matt said, and Takeo nodded in agreement.

"I don't want to separate from the group," Zoron argued.

"Please," said Takeo. "You know what we must do."

Ultimately, Zoron conceded. Some of the villagers stayed, and some of the Kobbads also remained to help Matt and Takeo.

Suddenly, the thuds of something coming near got

louder, and great roars echoed throughout the rainforest. Up in the trees, the Kobbads shot their arrows to try to slow down whatever might be coming. Zoron looked back and shook his head. He had a feeling it was something big, and that it weighed a lot.

He was right. It was Goron, the large gorilla, twice the size of a normal one, and with six arms and two legs. He was as powerful as any beast.

They heard something from the opposite way—a loud roar—as well.

"Oh shit," Matt said.

"This is not good," Takeo responded.

Zoron had told them about Goron and Tigerman.

"We're in serious trouble," Matt said. Takeo nodded in agreement. They never thought that the two great forces would arrive together.

"I'll try to find a way to contain Goron," Takeo said.

Matt had an idea. "We need to try to make them fight each other."

"Yeah? How do you plan on doing that?" Takeo asked.

They stood all around like prey in the middle of the forest, Matt facing one way, Takeo facing the other. Matt was facing the direction Tigerman was coming from, and Takeo was facing the direction that Goron was coming from.

"Tigerman might be easier to contain," Matt offered.

They both looked at the Kobbad warriors, who shook their heads no. Matt and Takeo then both attempted to hide, as that was what they had suggested. The Kobbads had been working on traps while Zoron was arguing with Matt and Takeo. They had the rainforest at their disposal, and they quickly tied a rope to a very large log and raised it up in a tree. They anchored it like a battering ram and faced it toward the direction that Tigerman was coming from.

Tigerman, with his accelerated speed, reached Matt quickly, and the Kobbads launched the log, letting go of the rope that was held in the tree. The large log swung as Tigerman came out from the bushes and leaped into the air to attack Matt. The attacking Tigerman didn't see the log until after the missile had been launched. The brutal collision sent Tigerman flying.

Having been focused on Tigerman, Matt and Takeo now turned to see Goron. He hit both of them and sent them flying. The Kobbads quickly started firing arrows at the monster, but they seemed to have little effect on him. He swung his mighty arms and roared with tremendous anger.

Matt and Takeo landed on the ground quite hard and were in great pain, but they had no time to worry about that. They got up as quickly as they could. Matt spotted Tigerman's battle-ax peeking out from under some leaves and picked it up. He had it held tightly in his hand when Goron came at him with vicious punches. Matt ducked and jumped aside as much as he could. He sprinted like a man running for his life, jumping over logs and watching for anything that would cause him to trip.

Takeo found a large log, which he split into two pieces. He grabbed one of them and yelled at Matt to duck, then jumped out from the shrubs and swung the large piece of the log, splitting it across Goron's large head. Goron fell to the ground, stunned.

Matt jumped at him and swung the ax, cutting off his

first right arm. The beast roared with a cry that would wake the dead. Meanwhile, the Kobbads shot arrows at Goron, and some of them jumped down from the trees. The villagers saw a handful of skeleton warriors come in, so they joined the fight and let Matt and Takeo deal with Goron.

As the animal slowly got up, blood poured from his wounds. One of the villagers tossed Takeo a large spear that was as long as a javelin. He ran at Goron, nailing him in the gut with the spear. Goron roared again.

As the battle raged on, Tigerman reappeared. He began to leap with a tiger's clear ability and strength in his hind legs, right toward Takeo. Matt reacted and pulled Takeo down, out of harm's way.

"Wow. Thanks," Takeo said gratefully.

Goron stood up with the spear still sticking in his gut. Tigerman leaped, and his body collided with the spear. Tigerman was soon dead, as the spear had killed him and made Goron fall to the ground. The Kobbads battled the skeletons, which fell one by one, as did some of the lizard warriors. By the end, each side had its share of warriors who died during the battle. It was a fight for life, and all that mattered was survival.

Matt retrieved the ax that he had dropped and gave it to Takeo. As the last skeleton warrior fell, Matt and the others all began to cut away the vines hanging in the rainforest. With Tigerman still attached to the spear, they tied down his feet. As Goron slowly pushed him off, the Kobbads and the village people tied his feet down with the vines—not an easy task. Takeo saw him struggle. His arms were loose, and though he only had five, he still used his strength to throw as many warriors aside as possible.

The Kobbads and the villagers were Goron's main focus. He had stopped looking for Matt and Takeo. Takeo, taking advantage of Goron's distraction, held the ax and crawled on the ground so that Goron wouldn't see him. When he finally reached him, Takeo stood up, and with one mighty swing of the ax, severed his head. Takeo dropped the ax and fell to the ground. He and Matt were sorely hurt and beat up. It was not a pleasant feeling.

Takeo rested, as did the others. Matt sat on a nearby log and looked over at the bloodied Takeo, shaking his head. Takeo saw the same thing, as he looked back at Matt. Matt put his hands on his knees. He knew that they had to get up and find Zoron and the mighty Gore. They were so close. They had to find the one who had helped them.

"It's almost over," Takeo said.

"I really hope so," Matt responded. "We need to find the hobbs plant and get back to Japan with it."

Matt and Takeo started to hustle after the Kobbad warriors and the village people.

"So, who is left?" Takeo asked.

Matt shrugged his shoulders. "I don't remember. Do you?"

"No, I really don't, my man."

"Well, we'll find out soon enough," Matt said.

Matt and Takeo were still a way off from the mighty Gore and Zoron, but they had heard fighting, and they knew they had to be coming close.

Sure enough, as Matt and Takeo ran, they saw Zoron in

the distance. Zoron knew it was them because he had heard their feet through the bushes and heard their voices as well. They were finally behind the big warrior.

"So, you two lived to see another day," he said with a big grin, his sharp teeth evident in his ugly face. Matt and Takeo found him hideous and disgusting.

It was time to make their move. They wanted to charge Giant Man, an eight-foot giant who was dressed all in black metal. He was an evil warrior, one of the last to protect the Amazon temple. Overcoming him wouldn't be easy. No one had ever made it past him into the temple. That was why bones lay around the temple—bones of people who had attempted to get the temple's treasures, who had failed in doing so.

Matt asked Zoron what he was waiting for. Zoron pointed at something very large up in the sky. As all of them watched, a huge shadow flew over the temple. The gargoyles were watching, too, and so was the dark giant.

Matt watched, more impatient than usual. He was itching for action, but as he watched, he began to feel a sense of calm take over. As they all watched, the gargoyles went after the creature. They were strong, but they couldn't overcome him. Finally, the watchers heard a noise that only a dragon could make.

Zoron turned to Matt and Takeo. "How did The Master's dragon come back?"

Matt and Takeo gave puzzled looks. "What do you mean, 'come back'?" Takeo asked. "What dragon? He has a dragon?"

"The red dragon that roars in the sky—how did he make it all the way here?"

"I have no idea," Matt said. "I've never seen this dragon before."

Zoron said, "Well, I have, and I thought he had been killed, but now I see that he is still alive. He is meant to belong to The Master."

As they watched, one by one, the three gargoyles came crashing down from the sky. One landed in the Amazon, and the others landed in front of the large, evil Giant Man. The gargoyles were extremely hurt, with large claw marks and gashes from the fight in the sky.

Wearing red armor almost the same color as his scaly skin, the red dragon flew down right in front of the temple. The Giant Man ran at the tall dragon with his sword. The dragon's two large horns on top of his head and the one on his snout made him look extremely scary, and the claws on his feet showed that he could not be hurt by much.

They all had their weapons ready to fight.

Zoron looked at Takeo and Matt. "Funny, I don't remember him being that big before."

Takeo and Matt looked terrified.

"He got a lot bigger," Zoron confirmed after a long look.

All of Giant Man's black armor couldn't have saved him from what came next. The red dragon reached for him and with the snap of his neck, it bit his head cleanly off. Giant Man was now dead.

The red dragon called for Matt with a booming, raspy voice. "MAAAAAATT!"

"How the hell does he know my name?"

"Red dragons are magical dragons," Zoron explained.

Shaking with fear, Matt walked toward the dragon. Everyone else was just as scared that he knew Matt's name.

The red dragon looked down at him and started to talk. Matt hadn't expected that.

"Are you Matt Rider?" The dragon leered at him.

Matt nodded.

"What is it that you seek?"

"The death of The Master," Matt answered.

"You dare try to kill him?" The red dragon slammed his foot down angrily. "He is not your concern anymore."

Matt looked at him and asked, "Why not?"

"There is a new evil," he said.

"A new evil?"

Takeo had a puzzled look on his face as well.

"Who is the new evil?" Matt asked.

"Nemesis," the red dragon answered. "He is your concern. The Master has done much to change from what I have observed. All I can tell you is that he is better for it."

"So, where does that leave me?"

"Are you forgetting about the other ones?" the red dragon asked.

"The other ones?" Matt looked puzzled.

The dragon named those from New York. "It leaves you where you want to be left. You two need each other, and you have to trust each other if you both hope to succeed. It won't work if you don't. I will wait here. Go in the temple and get the hobbs plant."

Matt couldn't believe he'd just had a conversation with

a red dragon, and that the dragon knew so much about everything.

Matt and Takeo entered the creepy temple, and they didn't have to go far before they found the hobbs plant growing everywhere. Matt grabbed as many of the plants as he could. They didn't know how many they were going to need.

Zoron followed them into the temple and handed Matt a bag that the villagers had made from leaves. It was a strong bag that would hold a lot of hobbs plants. They threw in as many as they could grab, and they were soon done their task. They left the temple, rubbed the mighty Gore's head, and shook the very large hand of Zoron.

The red dragon put his head down on the ground. "It is time to go."

After a moment's hesitation, Takeo jumped on his back, and Matt got on as well.

Zoron asked them to wait. "What about the Core? How do we destroy it?"

"Ah, the Core," the dragon answered. "The Core is a device that only the most powerful of beings, whether with technology or strength, can destroy."

Zoron looked at him. "So, The Master has to do it?"

The red dragon said, "The Core was sealed long before his time, and he knew nothing of it. He has no idea what the Core is." The red dragon looked at Zoron and continued speaking, with a tone of warning. "Watch for Aramids. He is the dark lord among the dark lords. He is twenty times more evil than The Master will ever be. His red dog Akides has been roaming around the site of the Core. It has been said he is back, too. Watch for him and protect the homeland. His dark lords are coming, and his army. The Core is by the end of the Amazon River that meets the Nile River."

Zoron waved goodbye, and with that, he headed back to the village.

~~~

The red dragon, with Takeo and Matt on his back, flew right up to the Temple of Time in Japan. Matt and Takeo quickly ran into the temple's war room. The eighth and final wizard, Radagast, was one of two who were still alive. The others' spirits had gone up to the gate, where they worked hard to keep the peace in the world. These wizards had held on, but the glass had only a little time left.

Matt and Takeo opened the bag with all the bright yellow-orange hobbs plants. Then they did what the wizard instructed them to do. Matt looked for a cup that he had left at the temple during his previous journey. He saw it on the floor and picked it up. He took out a small drinking cup that he had in his backpack. Matt and Takeo squeezed each of the plants, trying to get whatever was in the hobbs plants into the cup.

Matt ran to the seventh wizard and gave him some of the liquid. He came around shortly thereafter. Then they got the medicine to Radagast. Both wizards gradually recovered, but they were extremely weak from having been poisoned for so long. They graciously thanked the two men for saving their lives.

Matt and Takeo said they were sorry that they had failed.
~~~

The eighth wizard spoke. "You didn't fail. We are alive because of you."

"But the other six died because we didn't make it in time," Matt said.

"You did your best. We are both weak. We must rest."

"Wait," Matt said to the wizard. "We must know some things."

"Ah, yes, it is my duty to tell you, since you saved at least one of us. Well, there is a war coming, and yes, you must trust The Master. I cannot help you this time. My battles are over. You two have taken on the great responsibility of joining the fight for this greater cause. You both will face things that you have never expected to face. But you will need to rely on The Master. He is the key to saving Earth."

"Earth?" Takeo looked puzzled, as did Matt. "What do you mean?"

"I mean exactly what I said. You must destroy the two Cores in order to save the world."

Matt said, "Two? I thought there was only one."

Radagast said, "No, there are two. The other is at the bottom of the Black Sea. But I wouldn't worry about that one, since your ally is going to destroy it. The Master is lying at the bottom of the Black Sea." He used some of the magic he had left and showed where The Master lay by opening a small viewing portal in the air around them that shimmered and revealed the image of The Master. He was in front of a giant water kingdom. "He is fine, but the people aren't. The main Core is in the Amazon. But be prepared to help The Master in the near future. You will need his help more than he needs yours, and you both have to make the right decision.

It is the way it has to be. I must rest now." With those words, Radagast disappeared, along with the other wizard.

Matt and Takeo, after absorbing what they had seen and heard in this revelatory moment, walked out of the Temple of Time, armed with their new information.

"Yikes, I forgot how cold it is here," Takeo said.

"We need to get home," Matt replied.

Both of them looked as if they had been through hell. They had a long journey ahead of them, not to mention that Matt had a wife back home who was probably going to kill him. He said as much to Takeo.

Takeo didn't feel bad for him whatsoever. He began to joke. "Well, that is on you," he said. "I'd hate to be in your shoes as police commissioner, when you get home and all the speculation hits the New York papers."

Matt cracked a smile. "Great entrance on a red dragon, as well. That will definitely make headlines."

Matt and Takeo were having some good fun, some much needed levity during a stressful situation.

~~~

The red dragon flew Matt and Takeo from Japan to New York and landed right in Times Square. The dragon was tired from the long flight. Matt thanked him, and Takeo told him to rest.

"There's an island in New York Harbor called Ellis Island," Matt said. "It has a big statue. You can go rest there."

Matt looked like hell, and so did Takeo. But it was midafternoon—time to go to the station.
~~~

They walked in and greeted everyone, and all who were present were overjoyed to see them. It gave them a sense of comfort. Of course, everyone had so many questions about where they'd been and what was going on. They explained that they would fill them in later. Matt and Takeo were happy to be back, but they both were tired, and a long sleep was in order for the two strong men. The day for talking could come later.

Chapter 8

The Master lay in the Black Sea. As many boats passed by, the waves moved his body and eventually forced him down to the very bottom of the sea. The Master hit the bottom, landing in front of a dark cave. He couldn't see anything but darkness. The fish that swam there always swam as fast as they could when they got to the front of the cave. It was as if they knew something sinister lurked there.

Indeed, something sinister did. A water dragon lived in the deep, dark cave. A blue dragon—half dragon, half octopus—it had the body, strength, and scales of a dragon, and the tentacles of an octopus.

The Master eventually got up and opened his red eyes. He noticed bubbles coming out of the cave and went in to investigate. He heard the roar of the water dragon and drew his swords. "I am The Master!" he cried. "Who goes there?"

The water dragon charged with great speed, but he halted right before he would have hit The Master. He seemed to understand who The Master was inherently and showed some respect for him.

"Who are you?" The Master asked.

"I am a legendary dragon named Montazoma. I live as guardian of the water kingdom, hiding and keeping the water kingdom safe. But recently, I have noticed different serpents and sea creatures coming out of this great portal."

"What portal?" The Master asked.

"Come. I will show you."

The Master climbed on Montazoma's back, and they glided through the water to a portal that had opened only a few days before. As they sat on a cliff near the water kingdom, The Master said to his new acquaintance, "No one knows I'm here. Let's go back to your cave."

Montazoma swam back quietly, hiding from the water kingdom warriors. He looked at The Master. "Even as strong as you are," he said, "you can't destroy the Core by yourself. You can kill the people of the water kingdom, but you can't destroy the Core. It is said that there is only one thing that can destroy the Core. Legend has it that it is Oman's sword."

"I've heard of Oman's sword," said The Master, "but I thought that sword was only legend."

"No, it is real," Montazoma assured him. "It hasn't been seen for centuries. The great power within the sword is legendary. Only a special person can hold that sword. Many people have tried to hold it, and the sword has denied many in return. With you, on the other hand, it would be perfect unity, I'm sure of it. No human can hold that sword as you can. You fight for your own cause and are most powerful with a sword in your hand. That is why once you find it, you will be more powerful than anything. You yourself will be a weapon. You will be able to destroy the Core. I truly believe this."

"The Core is that powerful?" The Master's eyes widened as he considered the possibilities.

"Yes, it is a force so powerful that nothing can touch it or go near it. Only the creatures that come out of it can pass through it without getting hurt."

"Well, then, if I can't destroy it now, I'm going to take out that kingdom."

"You are going to take out that kingdom?" Montazoma started to laugh. "That is really funny," he said. He looked at The Master. "This isn't your environment. You are underwater."

"Yes, but I can adapt to anything. I've been underwater for well over the time that I should've been, and I'm still here. Where is the water kingdom?" He spoke with resolve and a gleam in his eyes.

"I really don't want you to do this by yourself. There are far too many of them that can hurt you."

"I can't be killed. I have a power that can't be matched by them."

"Well, then, you must learn about Gafnor," Montazoma said.

"Gafnor? Who the hell is he?" The Master asked gruffly.

"He is the great leader who controls all the sea life underwater, and he can use everything in the water to kill you."

"Well," The Master said, shrugging, "he can try to use everything, but don't forget: I am dead. I can't be killed." He paused. "Go back into hiding. It is time that you don't fear anything."

"Kill Gafnor, and the sea life will not be cursed," Montazoma said. Then he reminded, "But you still need the Sword of Oman to destroy the Core."

Montazoma swam and dropped The Master at the farthest point from the water kingdom.

"Good luck," he said.

The Master rubbed the top of the water dragon's snout and headed back to the cave. His two swords in hand, The Master walked and walked. He knew what he was going to be in for. He finally approached what seemed to be a large city, a kingdom of the sea that the water monsters ruled. He knew what he was walking into. At least, he hoped he did.

~~~

The skull warrior was recognized by a few Zion warriors. The Zion people were the race who ran the underwater kingdom. Everything was bigger and meaner there beneath the sea. When they saw him, the sea horse monsters commanded him to halt.

The Master had his two swords out. Many warriors surrounded him, and he was informed that he was under arrest for trespassing under Gafnor's command.

The Master laughed at them. "That's funny," he said. "Me, trespassing? You're out of your minds."

The Master surveyed the Zions. They all had long hair down their backs, and clothes that wrapped around some parts of their arms and legs. They carried glowing
~~~

red swords, their backs were arched with fins, their bluish-green skin shone, and their claws were very sharp. They wore body armor that covered their chests and left their stomach exposed. Their feet had nothing on them.

"Who are you?" one of them asked.

Looking at the Zions surrounding him, he responded, "I believe sushi is on the menu." The Master held his swords in both hands and started twirling around in a circle.

The Zions all drew their weapons.

The Master went faster and faster. He went so fast and was so deadly that he killed everything in his path, dicing and cutting it into pieces. He went after all of them—the warriors themselves and the sea animals they rode. It was crazy how fast he spun, how quickly the Zions flew, and how many he killed in a short period of time.

From his throne room in the castle, Gafnor watched everything transpire. Frustrated, he slammed down his fist. With his long hair and his body armor, he looked like a mighty warrior. "Who is he?" he shouted to the palace guards. "Get me something on this guy."

One of the guards ran to find out what he could about The Master.

The Master, who could do anything, had easily heard what Gafnor asked, and he wasn't even near the throne room.

"I am The Master," he shouted at him. "You will die today."

Gafnor, part of the Zion race, had their innate great sense of hearing. The Master stood in front of the large kingdom, and the guards all sat on top of the castle, shooting their guns and crossbows and anything they had at The

Master, including water grenades and machine guns that were typically made for a water race. No matter what they shot at him, he still walked. He acted as if he were used to getting shot at and remained unaffected and undeterred.

The Master stood directly in front of the castle. He saw that there was no way of getting inside. He held his swords, one in his left hand and the other in his right hand, and flung them up in the air. One sword went up toward the right side of the castle, and the other went to the left side of the castle. The Master watched as the swords went along the top wall, going after all the warriors who guarded each side of the castle. Each sword swung and sliced and diced each warrior who was up on each post, leaving many bloodied and bleeding the color green.

The Master hadn't been in the kingdom long, and already his power had proven how great he was. The swords came directly back to The Master, and he put them in the scabbards on each side of him. Then he put his hands together, almost as if he were making a temple with them. A large crystal came out, then another and another and another, followed by what seemed to be hundreds of them. The Master let them go, and the castle had its doors blown off. Mini explosions all over the castle did crucial damage, and many of the Zions fled.

The Master walked extremely slowly with his two swords back in his hands. He was angry and determined in his stride. He was resolved to give the blue dragon a piece of his mind—for a little bit, anyway.

Zion soldiers with daggers and other weapons swarmed out the front of the castle and swam at The Master as if they wished death upon him. The Master stood there as if he didn't care. One by one they attacked, and all received the same result: a slice from the sword or a kick that damaged their vulnerable bodies. Some got a kick to the stomach, and some had their skeletal system crushed. Their fear steadily intensified. Who wouldn't be afraid, fighting a man with a skull as a head? It wasn't every day that they saw this in the underwater cove.

The Master made quick work of them. It was way too easy. As he finally got to the front and through the doors, he saw that the castle had suffered major damage. He found more Zions waiting for him, some twenty to thirty. He had a great battle ahead.

They had spears and attacked him fiercely. The Master used his mighty hands and feet as more and more came to aid the effort against him.

Meanwhile, Gafnor knew The Master was inside, as he watched with his four great warriors in the throne room. He couldn't wait for The Master to fight his guards. Gafnor knew that this warrior might have the chance to kill him and his monsters.

The Master had his two swords in his hand. They were his trusty best friends that he always carried. His skill was far beyond anything that anyone could control. He was truly the master of his swords.

The skull and his eyes were lit a pure red, and the fire burned in the water. It was as if the rage in him would not end, and even the water couldn't stop it from burning. The Master set his sights on killing all the Zions, and he was ready for Gafnor.

The Master seemed to be changing his ways, becoming

the image that Glenn had seen of him in Transylvania. The Master didn't want to be what everyone saw him as. But since he had destroyed Midtown Manhattan, it would be hard for people to change their view of him. Nevertheless, the way he had been perceived was gradually changing.

The Master stood in the middle of the castle, and all the Zions surrounded him. The castle was already falling apart, with pieces of the water kingdom destroyed, and battered and dead bodies were strewn all over. There was nothing that hadn't been destroyed. This made Gafnor enraged at The Master. Gafnor had only known him by his name, and he was far more powerful than Gafnor had even judged him to be.

The Master looked around, turning his head slightly to the left and then slowly to the right. All the Zions were terrified, and he could smell the fear in them. It was quite easy for him to discern. He finally was in battle mode.

It was The Master's time to be a hero. He was the one person connected to all of this. Little did he know that his journey to become a hero was just beginning.

The Zions began to swing their daggers and their weapons of choice. The Master was only one, and there were many Zions he had to avoid. It was nothing like avoiding the warriors on the mountains in Japan. These Zions were many. As one got killed, three more would come. The Master was quicker and much more agile, and his hands and feet were like accessory weapons. The Zions' bodies were fragile. It didn't take much of a hit from The Master's mighty arm or leg to cause major damage or put them within inches of death.

Most Zions thought the best hope for Gafnor to live would be to run. Even if Gafnor did die, there was no way that The Master was going to destroy the Core. The gory battle took time, and nothing slowed The Master down. The Master killed all the Zions without getting hurt, and his swords were covered in green blood from the dead bodies that lay all over the entrance to the water castle.

As The Master searched every room of the elaborate castle, he found treasure upon treasure broken and destroyed. There was nothing but pure destruction left in his wake.

The Master came into the main room and saw a door that wasn't open. Bubbles were coming from underneath the door. It wasn't from his breathing, either. What could be waiting for him? What was it that Gafnor had in store for him now?

He took a few steps into the room. It appeared to be the throne room, though the Prince was gone. As the door slammed shut, a huge arena appeared as if by magic. It looked as if it was from the time of the Roman Empire, only it was prepared for a death match in water. The Master stood in the middle of the arena, and Gafnor sat and applauded, as did the other people of the sea.

Gafnor, with his light green appearance, turned toward him. "You won't live past today."

"No, *I* will live, and *you* will die," The Master declared, correcting him.

As the audience clapped, four mighty water-rock soldiers came crashing down from the sky. They were built from pure water rocks and were as big and strong as most anything. When Gafnor saw The Master run at them, he knew he didn't fear anything. Gafnor had never seen a warrior so vicious, evil, and powerful as The Master.

Aramids had some contact with Gafnor, and he knew this was their only chance of getting rid of The Master. Aramids, the darkest lord of them all, knew they had to make their stand against The Master here while they had the opportunity. The Master was far stronger than any of them, and he could be the one to stop them all. Therefore, Gafnor had to stop at nothing.

No matter what he threw at him, The Master kept on coming and coming, tireless and tenacious. He was an indestructible force. Gafnor had never seen anyone like this. Even the great Aramids worried when he witnessed the great presence of The Master. Aramids had known of his reputation, and what one person like him was capable of doing. His existence alone could ruin the plans to take over the world. It would only be a hindrance to have him around.

The Master, resolute, began to fight the water-rock soldiers. They were like very large and bulky rocks. They had mighty fists, wore a buckle at their waists, and had green helmets on their heads. They were powerful enough to give The Master problems. The Master had to contend with four of them at once.

One of the water-rock soldiers punched The Master through the arena door and out into the entrance hall. The Master lay on the floor for some time, stunned. He eventually got up and dusted himself off. He started to run toward the door, and as he did, his body shaped itself into a rocket and sped lightning-fast right into the arena, going through the first water-rock soldier and destroying him.

Pieces of the soldier went flying up into Gafnor's face, and he realized that his water-rock soldiers were not going to defeat The Master as easily as he had hoped, if at all. The audience moaned as all the other monsters looked on. The Master wanted to end this quickly, so he put his palms up, and his size increased so much that he was twice the size of the other two water-rock soldiers. He stepped on them and crushed them both. After that, The Master shrank down to size and began to fight the other water-rock soldier. As the water-rock soldier threw punches with his large fists, The Master caught his hands and blocked them. The Master punched him straight in the face and repeatedly gave him hard kicks to the body and the head. Each kick broke some rocks, and then some more. The Master was like a wild dog with a bone, relentless in his nonstop attack. He wouldn't stop until the water-rock soldier had no fight left. As strong as he was, he was no match for The Master.

The Master approached and climbed up the podium from which Gafnor looked down upon him. He grabbed Gafnor and threw him right into the fight pit.

Gafnor, for his part, was not a great warrior. He was a tall, skinny figure with bluish-green skin just like the Zions, which he was one of. He had bandages wrapped around different parts of his legs, and long hair that stretched down his back in a ponytail. His hands resembled fish gills but had sharp claws. He had armor that stretched from his shoulders and chest. His face was blue and very distorted, as if it had been injured in a severe battle. Gafnor got up and ran toward one of the statues, grabbed a dagger, and ran toward The Master.

The Master looked at him. "This is truly unfair to you," he said. "I will put down my swords and not use them." The

Master put them in his scabbards and dropped them from his waist. He lifted his head and his eyes flared. He smelled the kill. He ran toward Gafnor as Gafnor ran for his life. No one in the arena was going to help him, either.

Gafnor swung his spear at The Master in a flailing motion. The Master ducked, then grabbed it and pulled it out of his hands and used it like a baseball bat. The Master swung the spear and hit Gafnor very hard, then threw it aside and broke it over his legs. He walked over to him, held the back of his hair, and repeatedly punched him in the face, until his face was covered in bluish-green blood. Then he threw Gafnor to the ground.

As Gafnor crawled weakly on the ground, trying to get away, he sideswiped The Master's leg, knocking him off his feet.

The Master laughed. From his position on the ground, he kicked Gafnor in the head, knocking him down easily. The Master stood up, and Gafnor lay on the ground. The Master grabbed him and began climbing up to the throne, pulling him with him. Once everyone saw where he was going, they all ran out of the arena. The Master slammed Gafnor into his throne repeatedly, and in the process, he broke the chair. The Master stood up over him and threw him into the water arena, and the throne chair as well.

The Master jumped down as Gafnor clung on for dear life. Though Gafnor was not a particularly good warrior, many hadn't lived to see another day when they had fought him. Gafnor got to his feet very slowly. The Master had been toying with him, and he knew it was only a matter of time. Gafnor's cape was ripped, and the bandages from his legs had begun to come off. The Master ripped them off and went behind him. He began to choke him. The Master relished the act. He kept at it until Gafnor was almost dead, and then he let him go.

Gafnor fell to the ground and laughed at him.

"Why do you laugh, when you know you are going to die?" The Master snarled.

"Aramids is going to kill you."

"Ha ha, funny," The Master responded. "I can't die, you idiot. I am immortal."

Gafnor looked at him, and his eyes looked as if they were going to come right out of his head. He got to his feet and began to run, but very slowly. The Master ran toward him, and as Gafnor tried to defend his point of attack, The Master broke Gafnor's arm with one kick. The arm hung from the bone as it popped out from its skin. Gafnor's gruesome screams were hard to bear. Gafnor was not too far from death. With one punch, The Master put a hole in his chest, exposing all his bodily organs. Gafnor was now dead.

The Master looked around for something to take as a souvenir but didn't see anything interesting or worthwhile. He then felt a strong vibration as the entire castle began to come crumbling down. The walls began to crash, and the floor cracked. The Master knew it was the same thing that had happened at Dracula's castle, so he grabbed his two swords and ran as fast as he could out of the water kingdom.

He got out in the nick of time.

As the blue dragon came out of hiding, he saw the last of the castle sink. He congratulated The Master for defeating Gafnor. As the castle sank, the Core appeared not too far from the water dragon's lair. "It's a new day, a new battle," the dragon said to The Master. "You can't destroy the Core without Oman's sword. I believe your work is done here."

The Master looked at him, not knowing how to respond.

"Whenever you need to get to New York, I will get you there," the water dragon continued to speak. "Use this instrument to call me. It is a talon flute. If you have this flute, you can call either one of us. You touch the color of which dragon you choose to help you. The blue dragon and the red dragon are now in your control."

The Master took the instrument, inspected it, and nodded at him in gratitude. "I'm going to Glenn's house next," he said.

"I know him. I don't think he's home," the blue dragon said thoughtfully. "Yes, I think he went out for a while."

The Master called for the red dragon instead, and the red dragon flew him to Glenn's house, then left as The Master went in to rest. Even great warriors needed rest, and The Master was weary from his long journey. Little did he know, it was far from over.

He went in and found a note beside the bed. It read, *Dear Master, we have gone on a journey, but we will meet up very soon. Glenn.*

He left the note on the table, lay down on the bed, and shut his eyes.

Chapter 9
New York

Matt got up in the morning after a long sixteen-hour sleep. Sherry was worried that he had slept that long. She didn't quite understand all the details of his journey with Takeo.

Matt finally got his slippers on and headed downstairs. Sherry settled next to the big muscle-bound man on the couch and gave him his coffee. Matt looked at her with real concern causing creases in his forehead.

Sherry started to get anxious. "What is it?" she asked. "You've never had a look like that on your face before."

"We're going to be in some serious trouble, Sherry," Matt responded. "I can't believe I'm admitting this. We're going to need The Master's help."

Sherry jerked away. "You're out of your mind," she said.

"Please listen to me," Matt implored.

"Matt, he almost killed you and Takeo, and he killed Captain Thomas. How can we forget that? And besides, where the hell have you been? The papers have been very cruel to you and Takeo."

Matt looked at the front page of the *Post* and read the headline: *Hopeless NYPD*. "Yes, I can tell. Well, you really want me to start? We'll be here for quite a while."

Sherry looked at him. "You'd better tell me."

So, Matt began to tell the story to Sherry, starting from the very beginning.

As he spoke, Sherry was amazed, but for some reason, she believed him. "How the hell are you going to stop these things from happening?" she finally asked when he was finished.

"I don't know," Matt responded.

"What ever happened to The Master?" she asked.

"I haven't seen him since our wedding day, the same as you," Matt said.

"How is that possible?"

"It just is. There's something that has to happen."

"What do you mean?" Sherry tried to make sense of the whole situation. "How has The Master not come back?" It had been two weeks since they had all left New York Harbor. It was a mystery. How could a monster like The Master have disappeared from the face of the earth? "Let's call Takeo and have him come over."

"That's a good idea. You go ahead."

Sherry went to the kitchen, picked up the phone, and called him. About forty-five minutes later, Takeo arrived with Curtis and Tonya. Jack and Jennifer pulled up behind them. Matt, still exhausted, answered the door in his sweatpants and let them in.

Ten minutes later there was another knock on the door. Matt sighed. "Who could that be?" He greeted a little old man dressed in funny-looking foreign clothes, standing alongside a woman dressed in similar fashion. It was the old-time traveler and his wife, but Matt had no idea who they were.

"My name is Glenn, and this is my wife," the old man said in an accent that was hard to place. He could have been from anywhere.

If Sherry hadn't believed him before, she believed him now. She now knew for certain that Matt hadn't made anything up.

Glenn pushed his way in with his old wooden staff, and his wife followed. She was a little smaller than he was, and they both looked as if they belonged to the dwarf family.

It seemed strange to all of them that the two were at Matt's house.

"Your soon-to-be ally knows who I am," Glenn said. "You must listen to me and listen very carefully. Things happen for a reason, and the reasons, I can't tell you. But a war is coming. You must protect yourself." He spoke somberly and with authority.

Jack looked at Glenn and said, "We defeated The Master once before, and we can do it again."

"He is not going to be your problem," Glenn responded. "You will have a greater problem."

"What will that be?" Matt asked.

"Staying alive."

They all looked at each other questioningly.

"I can't tell you what happens," Glenn said. "All I can say

is, stay close together. Two of you won't make it, and others will question what you could have done to prevent it." Glenn looked at Matt. "You must trust me. Above all, you must trust The Master."

Matt shot him a hateful look. How crazy the old man was. How could he know such things? Make such wild predictions? Yet something about his tone seemed as if he truly believed what he said, and Matt felt uneasy. There was an air of prophecy about him.

"I know he hurt a lot of people, and he hurt your city, but he isn't like that anymore. Not as much, anyway."

"We are not helping him, and that's that," Matt said firmly.

"Well, if you don't help him, your city will be worse off than when The Master leveled Times Square." Again, the old man spoke with conviction that was convincing.

"How do you know about that?" Matt asked.

Takeo jumped in. "Matt," Takeo said, "Glenn was there. He's a time traveler. They know everything."

Matt's eyebrows raised. Now things were falling into place. Curtis nodded in agreement.

Meanwhile, the girls had gone into the kitchen to get some refreshments, but from there, they could still hear everything. They were very interested in what Glenn had said.

They came back to the living room. Jennifer had some bagels and put them down on the end table. Sherry had coffee, and Tonya had a tray of pastries.

Tonya jumped into the conversation. "How are we supposed to trust The Master?"

Curtis put a hand on her shoulder as if to reassure her.

"You can see for yourself." Glenn took off his old cloak, which had a stink about it because it hadn't been washed for years. Sherry had to open the windows because it was so bad. Jennifer retched.

Glenn used his magic to project images of things that The Master had done—some good, some bad—on a wall in the house. The images showed how The Master met Glenn, and where he had come from, and what his purpose was. How The Master killed an ancient legend and freed the people from the fear of Dracula. How he fought Nemesis and thought to destroy him, until Albert used a rocket launcher on him. And, finally, how he destroyed the underwater kingdom.

"He has done a lot of things that none of you would've been able to do," Glenn said. Glenn also told the group the things Matt and Takeo had done in order to save the eight wizards, and about going to the Amazon temple and getting the hobbs flower.

"Yes, all of that was good and great, but you two had the easy things. There is a war coming. In order to be the hero, you will have to accept that this is not a fight you can win without The Master."

Matt and Takeo looked at each other, and then the rest of the group looked at them as well. Their unspoken words conveyed a great deal. They believed this strange old man.

"How can we not win this fight?" Takeo asked.

Glenn answered, "Out of all people, you know what is coming."

Takeo nodded, his countenance darkening, then said,

"The dark lords are coming." The Core had been broken by Aramids. Takeo wasn't sure who Aramids was, but his father and relatives knew who he was. "I've heard the name Aramids, but I don't fully understand who he is."

Glenn began to explain who he was and what his loyal lords could do.

Takeo sighed. "This is a war that has to be won by The Master. With The Master, not against him."

Matt didn't agree. Curtis looked skeptical as well, unsure what the right course of action might be. He and Tonya had suffered greatly at the hands of the fierce warrior.

Sherry looked at him. "You can't always be the hero," she said. Her tone was pleading.

"That brings me to my second point," said Glenn. "I am trying to help you, as things will happen a lot quicker than you think. If you get captured, follow your captors. Do anything they ask. You will find a way. But one thing I tell you: you will need to help The Master. Something will happen that you will have no control over, and all of you will have to get him back. This will be a team effort. He will be relying on you." Glenn got up and grabbed his cloak, a sense of finality in his words. His wife followed close behind him.

"Where are you going?" Jack asked.

"I have to help The Master locate his army and Oman's sword," Glenn answered.

"Oman's sword?" Curtis looked at Glenn questioningly, and a few of the others did, too.

"Isn't the story of that sword a legend?" Jack asked.

"Yes, and it hasn't been seen in centuries." Glenn opened the door.

"Wait," Matt said.

As Glenn turned around, Takeo asked, "What about the Core?"

"The Core? Aramids will control that. That's why I must locate that sword. Without that sword, the Core can't be destroyed."

Jack said, "The great and powerful Master can't destroy an energy door?"

Glenn turned around and hit Jack with his stick, causing him to cry out. "That Core is the darkness of the two worlds. The Core is too powerful. Once the seal is broken, darkness will overtake the planet until it is destroyed. There is nothing that can be done. Yes, it's true. The great and powerful Master won't be able to help." Glenn put his hat back on and took his stick in hand, and he and his wife walked out of Matt's house.

Matt looked at the others. "I was going to tell you guys all this, but I guess I won't have to. What do we do now?"

"We need to show you something," Jack said.

Sherry looked at him, as if she knew that things were going to get a lot worse before they got better. She knew Matt's brother could be reckless at times. Glenn had painted a picture in her head, and it wasn't a good one at that.

Matt asked, "What did you find out with Tonya?"

Before Jack could answer, Sherry asked, "Was it about that old subway line I asked you two to find in Lower Manhattan?"

Jack answered, "Yes, it was."

Matt looked at Tonya and Curtis.

She rolled her eyes. "Oh no, this can't be good. Let's go over there and check it out. We need this to be looked into."

"Why didn't you show this to me before?" Sherry asked.

"It was late, and I didn't want to disturb you and Matt."

"That's fine," Matt said. "No big deal. Let's go."

Matt drove into Lower Manhattan with the crew and parked his Yukon on the street with his emergency lights on. In the back of the truck were heavy guns and ammo.

"Anxious?" Jack asked.

"No," Matt responded. "Cautious. I don't take chances anymore." Matt looked at Jack. "And neither should you."

They all climbed down the old abandoned subway line and got down into the smelly sewer line. Matt and Jack had flashlights and some other things in the small bag that Matt carried.

Sherry saw Matt's concerned look. "What is it?" she asked.

Walking around in the old sewer wasn't something any of them truly wanted to do. The smell was gruesome, and what they were walking in was putrid. The water that had covered the abandoned train line for years probably had piss and other disgusting concoctions simmering in it.

Matt and the group walked around using their flashlights. Cobwebs covered the train car, which looked as if it hadn't been used for at least seventy years. It was dark and ominous to behold.

Jack tripped over broken rocks from the wall and caught himself. "What the hell is this?"

Matt shone his flashlight on the floor. "This is fresh," he said.

Tonya—still the pretty, big-busted, solid black woman—looked at the break in the wall. Curtis crowded in to have a look, and he gestured for everyone else to see what they did.

"That's no ordinary break," Sherry said. "There are teeth marks on it." She shrunk back instinctively.

Some gasps resulted from this declaration. The large claw marks and bite marks on the wall didn't leave a pleasant feeling in Matt's stomach. Deep down, he knew that Glenn was right, though he hadn't wanted to believe anything the old man had said. Aramids was the dark lord.

What Matt didn't know was that he carried a scepter that could move him wherever he wanted to go. Takeo and Matt had experienced some things, but nothing like what was about to come forth. Meanwhile, Sherry worried for her family and friends.

Matt and Sherry walked ahead, and Takeo, Jack, Jennifer, Tonya, and Curtis followed. From all over the sewer, they could hear loud laughter echoing. Was it some type of spirit? They realized it was something much more powerful than they wanted to believe.

An intense vibration shook the ground as they walked. It had to be Aramids. They were horrified at the thought of seeing him, but to see his three-headed bear named Mannor would have been just as terrifying.

The reverberations continued. Sherry stood beside Matt, and as scared as she was, Matt was equally scared, if not more so. He felt a great threat looming in his heart. The others gathered together behind them. When another huge vibration occurred, they ran without a second thought.

Whatever's causing the shaking must be something very large and very scary, Matt thought. As in the movies, things that gargantuan weren't usually too friendly, either.

As the others ran and got topside, Matt stayed and looked around, foolish cop that he was.

"You don't know what you are up against, Matt Rider," a voice said. "I am far worse than you can ever imagine. You want to see Hell? I *am* Hell."

Aramids slowly stepped into the light, and Matt looked up, horrified, at a ten-foot-tall red warrior who looked as if he were from Hell. He was as solid as a rock, built from head to toe without a single ounce of fat that Matt could see. He had two horns coming out of the side of his head, and he carried a large sword. He had gold bands around both biceps and smaller ones around both wrists. He wore blue shorts and a belt around his waist that had his name on it and a skull in the middle of it. His chest was bare. He wore black knee-high boots that had spikes on the bottom.

Scared for his life, Matt began to climb.

Aramids laughed, and Mannor roared with a sound so loud the volume of it made cars come to a stop in Lower Manhattan.

Matt made it to the surface, took off running, and joined the others in the Yukon.

As they drove away, with Matt at the wheel, Sherry said, "Matt, please slow down. Please slow down. Matt, dude, what did you see?"

Matt pulled over not that far from Penn Station, and began to hyperventilate. He was scared as hell. "Oh my God," he said, "this is way beyond anything that we've ever faced. This is going to leave us really screwed."

Takeo looked at him. "What do you mean?" he asked.

"This is what Aramids looked like." Matt started to

describe the ten-foot monster. It was like nothing that they had ever seen before. Matt said he was monstrous and terrifying, and he made the guys he and Takeo had encountered in the Amazon rainforest look like wimps. How was he or his team going to defeat anything like that monster? Matt knew he was way too powerful and far too gargantuan to defeat, or even hurt. Matt had so many residual bad feelings toward The Master, but he began to realize that everything Glenn had said was coming true.

"Why don't we try to find Albert?" Sherry suggested. "Maybe we can get Nemesis and try to reprogram him."

"That isn't a bad idea," Jack said.

Matt looked at them. "What, have you guys all gone mad? There's no way we can do that. He turned on The Master once before. Who knows if he'll turn on us?" But as they pulled up to the precinct, Matt relented, and gave orders for them to go to Chelsea Piers and find Albert. "Where you find Albert, you will find Nemesis."

So, Jack, Takeo, Curtis, and Tonya all suited up. Takeo had still been wearing his armor from when they had left on their journey. Jack drove, and as they approached the pier, they saw to their dismay that it was on fire. The ships had all been destroyed, and the smaller boats blown up.

Tonya called Matt, who was back at the station with Jennifer and Sherry. "We need backup. We need it now, Matt."

"Nemesis is working well, and probably a lot better than before," Jack said.

"Oh my God," Tonya said. "That's impossible. How the hell is he alive?"

Just then, a big eruption occurred in Midtown. As the cars drove down Thirty-Fourth Street, the concrete right in front of Penn Station started to rupture, and finally broke. Cars crashed into the hole. Other cars crashed into each other, and concrete went flying down onto the steps of Penn Station. People jumped out of their cars and ran as fast as they could, mobs of people racing and pushing each other out of the way. Many people got trampled. It was a mob scene like none the city had experienced before.

Then Nemesis emerged. Beside him, to their horror, sat an evil black bear, and on the bear's back was Aramids, the red demon warrior.

The shadows of darkness came within the city skies. It wasn't the darkness that came from The Master. The world had now fallen into the stages of darkness, with New York City being one of the three, along with the Amazon and Romania. Each area began to have similar events transpire. There was no sunlight, and darkness loomed as black as any evil heart.

The red demon warrior spoke. "Run, my human slaves," he said in his thick, deep voice. "Run as you may."

From all over New York, gargoyles flew in, attacking innocent people, clawing at them, and killing as many as they could. Skeleton warriors covered every inch of the city. They had bones and swords and shields, and they all surged in an attack on all humans. It was total mayhem and incurred a lot of bloodshed, as many suffered and died at the hands of Aramids. Aramids roared powerfully and lifted his scepter as he opened the final Core in the middle of Thirty-Fourth

Street. It was total devastation, destruction like nothing that had preceded it.

Meanwhile, answering the call for backup, Sherry, Matt, and Jennifer weren't too far from Chelsea Piers. They didn't know just what type of chaos would ensue, and if they had, they might have turned around and fled. Instead, unknowing, they ran toward the fray.

Chapter 10

Resting at Glenn's house, The Master awakened to a disturbance outside. He went to the door and found that the red dragon, Akatides, had landed.

"Aramids has control of everything," the dragon informed him.

The Master, incredulous, asked, "As in what?"

Akatides answered, "The world."

Without thinking twice or lingering to decide on a course of action, The Master simply reacted and got on Akatides's back, and they flew into the air.

As they left, skeleton warriors took to the sky, trying to stop them. They had been warned to kill at any cost, but Akatides and The Master were too hard to take down. They were perfect for each other. As Akatides flew, trying to dodge the arrows in the sky, The Master caught any arrows and flung them back.

The Master stood on Akatides's back and leaped from the dragon to a Vagan pterodactyl. The Vagan pterodactyls were warrior skeletons that did battle over the Statue of Liberty. Aramids had control over an army of them. The Master knew what he had to do. He jumped onto each Vagan's back, one by one, and threw each skeleton off. Akatides killed a few as well, and before long, they finally cleared the sky.

Akatides flew as fast as he could toward New York. He finally saw the darkness over the city. He continued flying over, looking for Matt and Sherry, even though he didn't have to. They were both caught off guard when they heard the roar of the dragon.

The Master saw Aramids by Penn Station, and as he had the power to locate anyone with his eyes, he saw that Aramids had been chasing Matt and Sherry. He had gotten very close to them, as had Mannor. Matt and Sherry were seconds away from being mauled by the three-headed monster.

As The Master saw that, he zoomed in on Akatides. Aramids and Mannor looked up and saw him. Aramids, with his fierce, dark-red face, wasn't happy to see The Master, to say the least.

"Get out of here, now!" The Master yelled a warning at Matt.

Matt was shocked at this turn of events, and The Master's verbal outburst, and in a flash, he rethought what Glenn had said.

"Save your brother. He is at Chelsea Piers. Bring lots of weapons, as he is down on the ground."

The Master got off the red dragon. The skull creature helped Matt and Sherry onto the dragon, and they swiftly took off for Chelsea Piers.

The Master now was on foot, and he was fast approaching

Aramids and Mannor. Seeing that Akatides had taken Matt and Sherry to Chelsea Piers, Mannor raced toward The Master with renewed purpose.

The Master had just saved them from being killed, and Matt was shocked. Glenn had been right about him after all. He could hardly believe it, but the proof was there in what had just happened.

As Akatides flew up in the air, he talked to both Matt and Sherry. "The Master has gone through significant changes. You truly should give him a chance. You're very similar, but yet very different. You do need to work together. You can't win the war without each other." The grim truth was undeniable. Their former enemy would have to become their ally.

On the ground, The Master stood face-to-face with Mannor, the three-headed bear that was as huge as anything. Aramids stood and watched as Mannor charged at The Master. Mannor smacked him hard with one of his paws, sending him crashing through the roof of an SUV. The SUV collapsed and became a compact vehicle.

The Master rolled onto the ground. When he stood up, Mannor, following Aramids's orders, went after him like a beast that wouldn't tolerate him being alive. The large black bear's sharp teeth dripped saliva, ready to be used on The Master. His black body itched for a chance to rip The Master apart, limb from limb.

The Master wasn't going to let that happen. Aramids couldn't quite understand The Master's great power. It was beyond comprehension how this great warrior had come to be. Aramids knew some things about The Master, but not as much as he would have liked to serve him as ammunition in this showdown. The Master was a great warrior, and no one person had ever stopped him. The Master aimed to ensure that his legacy would continue.

The Master walked and then started to run at Mannor, and the beast, with its heavy frame, ran toward him. They both leaped in the air. Aramids could see the beast's pure muscle. The Master jumped high enough to miss his bite, and in midair, grabbed the back of Mannor's neck and snapped it in two. Aramids watched in shock. Any other person, Mannor would have had a great feeding on, but not on this day, and not with this opponent.

As The Master landed, Mannor landed on his side, breathing heavily.

"No!" Aramids yelled.

The Master took out his sword and thrust it through the beast in a swift, expert motion, not hesitating in the slightest. The Master and Aramids saw his eyes fading. Indeed, The Master had killed the beast.

Aramids stood there and yelled, a barbaric and primal sound. The echo of his roar shattered windows that hadn't already been broken. Aramids pushed the cars aside and ran like a crazy man, his very large sword in his hand. The Master stood there grounded, took a deep breath, and then charged Aramids. As The Master jumped at him, Aramids caught him with his right hand, and The Master went flying through a building already weakened by the earlier destruction. It shook and came crashing down on him.

Aramids saw the rubble and knew there was no way The

Master could get up from that. "That's for Mannor," he said proudly.

As Aramids bent over to pick up his sword, he saw rocks begin to move. As he continued to look, he saw more movement. He blinked, incredulous. "What the hell? That isn't possible."

Flying faster than anything, out of the pile of rocks burst The Master. He lifted Aramids off his feet, held him by the waist, and ran, using Aramids's body to take out a series of light poles. The Master slammed him down on the concrete in front of Penn Station, then kneed him on each side of his head and began to repeatedly punch him with the spikes on his hands.

Aramids grinned as he got a few punches in. He picked The Master up and threw him off of him. But The Master was fearless, and he was in death mode, so nothing affected him. He was very hard to even hurt at this point. The Master got up, and as Aramids stood, too, The Master jumped on his back and repeatedly punched him in the side of the head with his spiked hands.

Aramids tried to grab him and throw him over his shoulder. The Master's grip was so tight, however, that no matter how hard Aramids punched the skull figure, it didn't hurt him. Even with his heavy fists colliding with The Master's skull, he remained unhurt. The Master hadn't stopped, and he would not relent or concede the fight.

Aramids finally ran The Master's back straight into a bus stop sign. The Master lost his grip and fell to the ground at last. Just as quickly, though, The Master got back up and kneed Aramids's face a few times. The Master grabbed his horns, and with his right hand, ripped one of them out of his head and stabbed Aramids with it in his right leg. Aramids roared in pain and fell to the ground.

The Master walked over and saw a metal light post lying on the ground. He picked it up and snapped it with both hands. Aramids was in a lot of pain. He had never fought anyone like him. The Master was a definite killer.

The side of Aramids's head, where The Master had ripped out the horn, gushed a greenish blood, and his face bled as well. The Master started to hit Aramids with the light pole as he lay on his stomach. Each whipping force was heavier and more brutal than the previous one. Aramids was in trouble. Skeleton warriors came to rescue him, and their arrival bought him some time to recover.

With even greater force, summoning strength from some unknown place inside himself, The Master battled some of the skeleton warriors, as others attended to their great leader and helped him use the scepter to get away. The Master finished off the skeleton warriors, but not before Aramids had transported himself to Chelsea Piers.

The Master found his swords, which he had dropped in Lower Manhattan. Things seemed to be worse there than when he had destroyed it, he noticed. After he picked up his swords, he didn't know where to go from there. He looked around for Aramids. As he looked up, he saw Akatides there instead.

"Come on," Akatides said. "Get on my back."

~~~
~~~

Matt and the crew were at Chelsea Piers battling the skeleton warriors. Moving in closer, Jack saw Nemesis. Matt again thought about what Glenn had said. Sherry had already seen what was going to happen.

Nemesis was using his guns and creating explosion after explosion. The pier was on fire, burning. It was quite a war zone. No one was safe.

Jack hid behind some wooden crates and a large trailer. Matt, Tonya, Curtis, and Sherry were far enough back to avoid being hurt, but Jennifer wasn't. She was trying to help Jack. As Nemesis shot rockets out of his fingertips, Jack—seemingly in slow motion—turned to see the rockets leave Nemesis's fingers, and he realized what was going to happen but was powerless to stop it. A large explosion occurred right where Jennifer was, killing her instantly. Jack let out a cry of dismay and anguish.

Matt saw the sky open up just then and Aramids appear. Aramids landed on the trailer right above where Jack was. Jack looked up as the red demon saw him. Aramids grabbed Jack by the throat and took the large sword that he carried and put it right through Jack's chest. In one hand he held Jack as if he were nothing, and in the other hand he held the sword. The rest of the crew stood stunned, and Matt was speechless, unable to process what he was seeing before him, his own brother being taken from him in plain sight.

After Aramids killed Jack, he threw his body to the ground.

Catching up to them, The Master saw Jack's body drop into the burning water and came running, with Matt close behind him. The skull figure wasted no time. He ran toward

Aramids, intending to jump at him, but Nemesis tackled him and he fell to the floor. Nemesis started to hit The Master repeatedly, and he had already taken quite a beating.

Matt got up and couldn't contain himself. His brother had just been killed by Aramids, and he, Tonya, Curtis, Sherry, and Takeo couldn't do anything, as they soon were surrounded by skeleton warriors.

Albert stood on top of the trailer with the red demon, Aramids. Aramids saw him rub the scepter, and a large gateway opened in the strong wind.

The skeleton warriors captured Tonya, Curtis, Matt, Sherry, and Takeo, and made them surrender their weapons. The skeletons also made them watch as The Master fought back.

Then, The Master turned to see a swooping wind that pulled Akatides into a whirlwind up in the sky. The Master wanted to save him, and in a moment of weakness got distracted from his battle. As he let down his guard, Nemesis hit him very hard, and the wind took The Master up as well. It twirled faster and faster, until it had thrown The Master and Akatides back in time.

They vaporized completely and disappeared from the sky.

Aramids and Nemesis and Albert stood on top of the trailer at Chelsea Piers. They had gotten rid of The Master and Akatides. Aramids wore a large, satisfied smile, and he started to laugh heartily. As maimed as Aramids was, The Master was now out of their way.

In the ensuing aftermath, the city was placed on lockdown, and the citizens of New York trying to get out were being halted by Nemesis and Aramids. All types of demon creatures filled the city's five boroughs. They swarmed. They infiltrated. New York truly had no hope. The cops had been seized, and all citizens had been led to where Nemesis and Aramids were. All sizeable creatures had been ordered to destroy every bridge that provided a way into the city. Other monsters put barriers in front of the tunnels. They were trapped.

Matt had no idea what they were going to do. The Master was who he truly needed, and he lamented that he had trusted him too late, wishing he had been able to convey his gratitude for their newfound alliance. With the death of his brother Jack, Matt couldn't think straight. It was a great loss to him, and Matt was very angry. If he knew The Master, he would find a way back, somehow. He had done it before, after all. But now, being one of thousands in chains, Matt was captured, and it was going to be hard to do anything while in captivity. He felt powerless, hopeless, mourning the loss of his city, his brother, and his future, if The Master couldn't find his way back to do something.

Aramids and Nemesis were truly destructive together. They had total rule of the city. No one was getting in or out. And no one in their right mind was going to help. They were stuck in this situation until its rightful conclusion, one way or the other.

How far away was the end for Matt, Sherry, Tonya, and Takeo? Was time on their side, or was this just the beginning? Matt had more questions than answers, and he was too tired to try to find the solutions. Where did The Master get thrown to? How was this going to end?

It was something that they would find out in the near future.

filled the city's five boroughs. They swarmed. They infiltrated. New York truly had no hope. The cops had been ejected, and all citizens had been led to where Nemesis and Aranida were. All sizeable resources had been ordered to destroy every bridge that provided a way into the city. Other monsters put barriers in front of the tunnels. They were trapped.

Matt had no idea what they were going to do. The Master was who he truly needed, and he lamented that he had trusted him too late, wishing he had been there to convey his gratitude for their newfound alliance. With the death of his brother Jack, Matt couldn't think straight. It was a great loss to him and Matt was very angry. If he knew The Master, he would find a way back, somehow. He had done it before, after all. But now, being one of thousands in chains, Matt was captured. And it was going to be hard to do anything while in captivity. He felt powerless, hopeless, mourning the loss of his city, his brother, and his future, if The Master couldn't find his way back to do something.

Aranida and Nemesis were truly destructive together. They had total rule of the city. No one was getting in or out. And no one in their right mind was going to help. They were stuck in this situation until its rightful conclusion, one way or the other.

How far away was the end for Matt, Sherry, Tonya, and Tak? Was time on their side, or was this just the beginning? Matt had more questions than answers, and he was too tired to try to find the solutions. Where did The Master get thrown to? How was this going to end?

It was something that they would find out in the near future.

About the Author

Frank DeStefano a Long Island native, and a fan of the Science Fiction genre. A fan of varietey of generes of books and movies. A lifetime baseball fan as well.

CPSIA information can be obtained
at www.ICGtesting.com
Printed in the USA
LVHW090703230223
739752LV00006B/22